BACK TO LUKE
Kathryn Shay

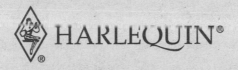

HARLEQUIN®

TORONTO • NEW YORK • LONDON
AMSTERDAM • PARIS • SYDNEY • HAMBURG
STOCKHOLM • ATHENS • TOKYO • MILAN • MADRID
PRAGUE • WARSAW • BUDAPEST • AUCKLAND

Recycling programs
for this product may
not exist in your area.

ISBN-13: 978-0-373-71579-4

BACK TO LUKE

Copyright © 2009 by Mary Catherine Schaefer.

www.eHarlequin.com

Printed in U.S.A.

"Hello, Luke."

Jayne cleared her throat and moved into the sunlight.

Every single muscle in Luke's body seemed to stiffen. For a moment he simply stood there, staring up at her. Jayne forced herself to hold her ground, despite the flinty look in his eyes that made her shiver.

"What the hell are you doing here?" he finally said.

"Eleanor invited me to stay with her."

"You can't do that."

Jayne squared her shoulders and lifted her chin. "Back off, Luke. I'm not as easily intimidated as I was when I knew you in New York."

"You ran, Jayne. Like you've been running all your life." Luke made a sound of disgust. "And I never knew you, lady. Never." With that he stalked away.

Dear Reader,

When I plan out a novel, I always think about the themes. *Back to Luke* deals with two primary themes: making mistakes then living with them, and what happens in a relationship when trust is betrayed?

Jayne Logan and Luke Corelli are flawed characters, which I like about them. Some bad things have happened to them and both have made one big mistake in their lives. They have to live with what they've done and promise to do better. Of course, they slip up.

Then there's the issue of trust. We all want to trust the people we love. And sometimes others don't live up to the faith we've put in them. Do I think we can regain another person's trust after betraying it? Yes. Do I think it's easy? No. Luke and Jayne find this out. Not only have they let each other down, but one of them does what he's promised he'll never do. To me, this situation is the epitome of trust. I've used it before, and when the betrayal occurs and the other person realizes what's happened, I often cry myself. Trust *is* fragile and can be broken at any time. What we do afterward alters the relationship and maybe our lives.

As for Luke and Jayne, their bumpy road to happiness is similar to all of ours, and I hope you can relate to each of them. Rest assured, there is a happy ending.

Want to learn more about me and my work? Visit me at www.kathrynshay.com. There are book trailers and a blog I update frequently. You can also see the blog at www.livejournal.com/kathrynshay. And you can connect with me on MySpace, at www.myspace.com/kathrynshay. Or write to me at kshayweb@rochester.rr.com.

Happy reading,

Kathryn Shay

ABOUT THE AUTHOR

Kathryn Shay is the author of twenty-four Harlequin Superromance books and nine novels and two novellas from the Berkley Publishing Group. She has won several awards. Among them are five *Romantic Times BOOKreviews* awards, three Holt Medallions, three Desert Quill awards and a Booksellers' Best Award. A former high school teacher, she lives in upstate New York, where she sets many of her stories.

Books by Kathryn Shay

HARLEQUIN SUPERROMANCE

908–FINALLY A FAMILY
948–A CHRISTMAS LEGACY
976–COUNT ON ME
1018–THE FIRE WITHIN
1066–PRACTICE MAKES PERFECT
1088–A PLACE TO BELONG
1123–AGAINST THE ODDS
1206–THE UNKNOWN TWIN
1253–OUR TWO SONS
1315–A TIME TO GIVE
1359–TELL ME NO LIES
1410–THE WRONG MAN FOR HER
1479–BE MY BABIES
1538–THE MAN SHE COULDN'T FORGET

To my good friend Eleanor Pierce, eighty-nine years young this month, who served as the model for the Eleanor in the book.

Thank you so much for all you've taught me and the time you've spent with me.

CHAPTER ONE

JAYNE LOGAN WAS a desperate woman. As she stood at the edge of the rest area overlooking Riverdale, nestled in a valley in Upstate New York, she admitted the stark truth to herself—she had no place else to go. Where people cared about her, anyway. Her life was in shambles, her parents were completely unsupportive, as usual, and over the years she'd alienated most of the acquaintances she'd managed to make.

Except for Jess Harper, her best friend from college, the man who'd been her lifeline in good times and bad. *Their* estrangement hadn't been her fault. She could still see him in front of his mother's house, tears in his eyes, six years ago.

I'll let you go, Jaynie. But only if you promise me one thing. If you ever need me, really need me, you'll call or come to Riverdale.

Well, she thought, shaking her head, she really needed him now—enough to risk what could very well be a powder keg of reaction from his wife, even after all these years. Naomi Harper's jealousy was the reason Jayne and Jess had cut off all ties and agreed not to see each other. At first they'd exchanged e-mails, then their contact had dwindled to cards at holiday time. In some ways, Jayne felt like she'd lost a limb when Jess and his mother, Eleanor, were no longer part of her life.

Pushing away memories of Naomi—they made her feel selfish for coming to town—Jayne got into the front seat of her rented Lexus and headed into Riverdale. Its population was about twenty thousand, but the place had the feel of a much smaller town. It hadn't changed much, either, she thought as she drove along Route 17 and into the heart of the city bisected by the Chemung River, with its quaint streets, old-school architecture and the glass factory's tall white tower. The edifice stood above the business area and blew its horn morning, noon and night, like a watchful parent guarding his children and calling them to work. Most of the townspeople had jobs in the factory or at headquarters, which she passed on the right. The beautiful black glass building rose up twenty stories, all sleek lines and interesting rounded corners.

Her heart began to thump in her chest as she turned off Sunset Boulevard and drove up Lexington Avenue, one of the many hills over which the population sprawled. She remembered when Jess had bought the big gray-shingled house on Second Street, near a park where his girls could play and surrounded by neighbors who had, of course, become his close friends. Everybody loved Jess and rightly so, given his generous nature and a sense of humor that could put anyone at ease.

Turning left, she pulled up to the curb and frowned. The house looked...shut down. She knew he still lived here. She'd gotten a Christmas card from him only four months ago. Damn it, she should have called. But she hadn't forewarned her friend of her visit because she hadn't been sure she'd actually come to Riverdale until she arrived.

Sliding out of her car, warmed by the April sun, Jayne took the concrete path to the sidewalk, climbed the first set of steps and the second. The front porch faced the entire valley and held a couple of lounge chairs; she noticed a small bike and a big-wheeled scooter tucked into the corner. They belonged to his girls. Suddenly, Jayne *needed* to see solid, family-man Jess more than ever.

She rang the doorbell. No one answered. The blinds were all closed and the house *felt* deserted. Because she was an architect, buildings were her best friends and she had a sixth sense about them.

"If you're lookin' for the Harpers, they aren't home."

Jayne turned to find a man on the sidewalk below. "Excuse me?"

"Jess and his family. They're gone." He smiled. "They went to Disney World. Naomi won the trip from the Glass Works. Needless to say, the kids were chompin' at the bit to get there. Jess took them on their spring break from school."

With a heavy heart, Jayne descended the two sets of steps, aware of the sounds of children playing in the yard next door and a lawn mower buzzing down the street.

The man had dark hair and eyes, and a kind smile. He held out a beefy hand. "Bill Parks. I went to high school with Jess. Now we're neighbors."

"Jayne Logan." They shook. "Jess and I were in college together."

His brow furrowed. "Did he know you were comin'?"

She shook her head. "I should have called." Now what was she going to do?

"You know his mom, Eleanor?"

"Yes, very well, as a matter of fact."

"She's still livin' up on Fifth Street. Might be nice for you to go see her. She's probably lonely for Jess. They took the girls out of school early for a two-week trip."

As she often did, Jayne wondered what it would be like to live in a small town and have everybody know your business.

"I'd love to see Eleanor." She reached for her phone. "Oh, wait, I don't have her number in my contacts list."

"I think she uses her cell now."

"Eleanor has a cell phone?" Jayne couldn't picture the older woman with modern technology.

"Yeah, no grass grows under her feet. You know the address?"

Never would Jayne forget the house Eleanor lived in. A stately three-story structure, it sported slate-blue siding, black shutters and huge porches that wrapped around the back and sides. And there were those beautiful gardens. Eleanor had taught Jayne everything she knew about growing things, and Jayne had missed the flowers and digging in the dirt when she'd moved to California, where she only had time for work and sleep. "Yes, I know where Eleanor lives."

The trip over to Chestnut Street and up to Fifth took only ten minutes. As she caught sight of the house, a rush of emotion flooded her. The place was as beautiful as ever, but something else caused her heart to swell and tears to spring to her eyes—memories of the time she'd spent here in Eleanor's loving care, having in Jess the brother she'd always wanted. Since they'd both been only children, Jess had felt the same way about her.

She parked at the curb, exited the car and hurried up a walkway flanked by pink and purple crocuses and sunny daffodils. For a minute, she just stood in front of the double front oak doors and laid her hand on the smooth, cool wood. Then she pressed the bell.

No answer.

Damn it.

Again, she rang.

Still, no answer. But contrary to Jess's house, this place was open and alive. Windows were raised on all three floors, allowing in the air, which in her mind had always meant the house was breathing in and out.

Maybe Eleanor was in the back, working in the gardens. She followed the brick path around to the rear and more of the flowers came into view, startling Jayne for a moment. So many colors. So many different varieties. Her favorites had always been the summer wildflowers, but Eleanor preferred the roses. Because it was April, other plants bloomed now. Jayne couldn't remember all their names but did recognize the snapdragons and the purple and white irises. The blossoms filled the air with sweet perfume like nothing man could manufacture in a lab.

Eleanor wasn't working on the beds, and though the shed door was ajar, Jayne didn't see anyone inside. She glanced up at the back porch. The door to the kitchen was open to the screen. With more anticipation than she'd had for anything in a long time, she climbed the steps and called out, "Eleanor, are you in there?"

No one responded. Jayne put her hand on the knob and had pulled the screen open a few inches when she heard behind her, "Hey there, darlin', what are you doing?"

The deep rumble of a male voice startled her and she jumped back as if she were breaking and entering. Her heart beating at a clip, she pivoted to find a man at the bottom of the steps. A big, half-naked man.

She was standing in the shadows, and he was in the bright sunlight, so it took a minute for her eyes to adjust. Oh, God, it was Luke Corelli! Someone she'd known a lifetime ago.

"Sorry, did I scare you?" His eyes narrowed. She couldn't see their color, but she knew they were brown, deep and rich to match the mane of dark hair on his head and whorls of it on his bare chest. It was a chest that at one time she'd explored intimately. Her gaze dropped lower to the nicely corded muscles of his legs and work boots on his feet.

A chuckle. "Like what you see?" he asked.

Dear Lord, he didn't recognize her. But why would he? She was a different woman, both physically and in personality, from the one he'd known twelve years ago when they'd both been twenty-six.

She cleared her throat and moved into the sunlight. "Hello, Luke."

Every single muscle in his body stiffened. For a moment, he just stood there, staring up at her from the ground; then, slowly, he climbed the steps until they were on the same level. Jayne wanted to inch back but forced herself to hold her ground, despite the flinty look in his eyes that made her shiver. Trying to conceal her reaction, she threw back her shoulders and faced him down.

Finally, he said, "What the hell are you doing here?"

LUKE STARED at the woman standing before him. Dressed in a tailored beige suit, she was taller than he remembered and her demeanor made her seem more confident and formidable than the eager junior architect she'd been over a decade ago when they'd hooked up in New York City. And, damn it to ever-loving hell, she was even more of a knockout now. Dark-as-midnight hair, cut short and feathery around a flawless face. He'd told her she had Liz Taylor eyes. Once, he'd fallen for their combination of innate sophistication and vulnerability. But no more. Never again.

"I asked you what you're doing here?"

Jayne Logan had wreaked havoc in Jess's family, something Luke had only found out about after she'd left him. Discovering that little tidbit made him understand why she'd insisted on keeping her relationship with Luke a secret from Jess.

"I'm here to see Eleanor."

"What, after you abandoned her? It was hard for Miss Ellie when you stopped coming to Riverdale."

Warmth and humor filled those violet eyes. "I forgot you called her that."

A small dog came running around the side of the house and flew up the steps. It was a beautiful little Yorkshire terrier with black and golden hair on a long leash. Bending over, Luke scooped the animal into his hands. "Shh…it's all right, Krystle."

"I see you're still living on the set of nighttime soaps."

Luke had a slew of sisters and, growing up, all of them had loved *Dallas* and *Dynasty*. As a hormone-crazed teenager, he got to watch Sammy Jo—aka Heather Locklear—every week, so he didn't complain.

"Forget about that." About everything he'd told her when he'd fallen like the proverbial ton of bricks for her.

"Explain to me why you're back in Riverdale after all these years."

She bristled and said, "That's my business," and nodded to the house. "Is Eleanor home?"

"No, she left for church right after I got here."

"That's right, it's Sunday."

"Don't go to church anymore?"

"No. You?"

Not since the course of events in his life had destroyed his faith in a Supreme Being. To some degree, the woman before him had been a part of those events. "No."

"What are *you* doing here?" she asked. "Last I knew you were in New York, making mega bucks. You said you'd never come back to live in a small town."

"I changed my mind." To avoid telling her why, to avoid explaining the worst thing that had ever happened to him, he gestured to the other side of the porch, walked over a few feet and turned the corner. She followed. "I'm building that for Miss Ellie. It's done, except for the painting."

"It's beautiful. I love gazebos. There's this really nice one in Paris in the—"

"Versailles Gardens. I know."

She cocked her head at him, a frown marring her brow. "You used to live overseas and traveled in Europe. I forgot about that."

Of course she had. This woman was very good at forgetting.

"How come Jess didn't build it?"

"For one thing, I like doing stuff for Miss Ellie and this is a gift from my whole family for her seventy-fifth birthday. Besides, it's already too much for Jess, trying to keep up with the flowers Miss Ellie can't get to, work, pitch in as Annie's soccer coach and do all the other things a husband and dad has to do."

"When will he be back?"

"End of the week."

Her eyes filled with something. Sadness, maybe, or was it fear? Whatever it was made them glisten like wet amethysts. And he remembered how the expression sucker punched him every time she got upset.

"Oh, dear."

"He couldn't have known you were coming." Luke's tone was gruff, and he had to shake off the kernel of reaction forming in his belly.

"He didn't." She nodded to the house. "Nor does Eleanor."

There was noise inside, and then Miss Ellie came to the screen, dressed in her Sunday best—a pretty pink suit, which set off her snow-white hair and still-sparkling blue eyes. "Luke, dear, I saw a Lexus parked out front. Did one of your female friends drive over to help you finish painting the gazebo?"

"Come onto the porch, Miss Ellie," he said gently.

Pushing open the screen, the older woman stepped outside and addressed the dog. "Hello there, Krystle. Having a nice time with Luke?" She glanced to the side and saw Jayne. "Oh. You must be a friend…" Her hand went to her chest. "Oh, dear Lord, Jaynie. *Jaynie!*"

Jaynie's face transformed from stone-cut marble to soft sandstone. "Hello, Eleanor, I…"

Suddenly, Jayne closed the gap between her and Miss Ellie and threw herself into the older woman's arms. From his vantage point, Luke saw Jayne close her eyes and hold on for dear life. The intimacy of their reunion made him feel like a voyeur.

Miss Ellie ran her hand over Jayne's hair. He remembered when it was longer and he could wrap it around his fist. "I'm so glad you're here," the older woman said. "I was praying for you just now in church, as I do every Sunday. God must have heard me today."

Still Jayne held on, as if she wasn't used to human contact.

Miss Ellie shot a worried glance at Luke. "Jaynie, are you all right?"

Jayne shook her head.

"Then you've come to the right place. Whatever it is, Jessie and I will help."

Luke could barely hear Jayne when she spoke. "I'm in trouble, Eleanor. Big trouble."

Oh, great, Luke thought. Not only had she abandoned Miss Ellie years ago, stirred up all kinds of things between Jess and Naomi, and ditched Luke without a second thought, now she was in *big trouble* and had come here to dump whatever it was on them.

Luke couldn't watch the scene before him so he left the porch and went back to the gazebo. Jayne's appearance in town had thrown him. But he knew one thing for certain. He'd learned his lesson twelve years ago and was sure as hell going to make sure Jayne Logan didn't take advantage of two of the people he loved most in the world.

CHAPTER TWO

BECAUSE JAYNE needed some time to collect herself, Eleanor had gone inside to make lemonade. Jayne walked around the house to a wrought-iron table and chairs. She slipped off the jacket she'd layered over a brown silk shirt and that was now making her warm. Draping it over the back of one of the chairs, she sat. From there, she studied the gazebo.

The whole structure was in keeping with the materials and the lines and angles of the main house. Black shingles matched those on the big roof, as did the slate-blue siding around the bottom half. She wondered what color he was going to paint the posts. They wouldn't be left natural, because he was up on a ladder priming them right now.

The noonday sun glistened off his sweaty skin, emphasizing his darkly tanned back and the breadth of his shoulders. God, she couldn't believe he was here, in Riverdale. She'd never even considered that he'd be back in town, or she most certainly wouldn't have come. When she knew him in New York, he and his friend Timmy had been making their first million, already at age twenty-six, and Luke had told her he'd never leave the big city. She wondered if Timmy was in Riverdale, too. She'd have to ask Eleanor about him.

The older woman exited from the side French doors and set down glasses of lemonade. Jayne was glad for the distraction from Luke. "Now, tell me everything, dear."

Jayne began simply. "Do you remember when I sent you the pictures and newspaper clippings of one of my buildings? The Coulter Gallery of Antiquities?"

"Yes, it's lovely. So innovative and well designed."

"Maybe not so well designed. The walkway that circled the interior of the building just…collapsed a few weeks ago." Every time she talked about this, Jayne's stomach clenched and her head began to hurt. "Luckily, there weren't any patrons in the gallery—it closes at nine and this happened about two in the morning. But many of the artifacts were destroyed."

Jayne shook her head, recalling the horrific phone call she'd received from the police. What had begun that day was a nightmare of epic proportions.

Ms. Logan? This is Chief Edwards of the LAPD. The upper walkway in the Coulter Gallery caved in. It did a lot of damage. Nobody was hurt, but we have a mess on our hands. The mayor said to contact your firm. We need the building plans and a consultation with you.

Bolting out of bed, she'd dressed hurriedly and sped over to the gallery. She'd never forget the sight of one of her babies maimed and crumpled into itself, or the smell of splintered wood and the light dusting of broken concrete filling the interior. Priceless artifacts, some of which were in now-smashed cases, some freestanding in the main area, were in shards. Later she would learn the astronomical cost of their ruin.

Eleanor's touch on Jayne's hand pulled her from the memory. "Oh, Jaynie, I'm so sorry. I know how important your career is to you. What caused the collapse?"

"We don't have the results of the investigation yet. And I keep going over the plans and racking my brain for what I might have done wrong. I can't find anything." She sighed. "So far, neither can the independent firm I hired to determine what happened."

"Then there's a good chance you *didn't* make a mistake."

"I'm truly hoping that, Eleanor. Meanwhile, I just have to wait."

"You'll do that here."

"Excuse me?"

"You'll wait for the board's findings in Riverdale with people who love you."

Stunned at the unconditional acceptance, Jayne couldn't speak around the lump in her throat.

Eleanor's gaze was knowing. There were few secrets between the Harpers and Jayne. She'd come to Riverdale on most of her college vacations instead of going to her parents' house because they were busy or traveling. "You went home first, didn't you?"

Jayne nodded.

"And your father wasn't supportive."

That was an understatement. It was the confrontation with Andrew Logan that had driven her from the Hamptons. He'd actually scolded her for having gotten herself in this situation and turned his back on her. She'd been foolish to go to him, to think that *this* time he'd be genuinely concerned for her welfare rather than her success.

"Jayne? What did Andrew do when you told him?"

"He wasn't happy with me at all. He thought I should go back to California and fight this."

"Could you do that?"

"No. They have my drawings, the specs from the contractors and the builders, and information from everyone else involved in the gallery's construction. They don't want any more of my input." She shook her head. "So I won't be going back to New York, either. The office closes for the month of May while everyone takes vacation. I usually go to my condo in Florida and sketch out some preliminary drawings for new projects before we get to them formally. I'll head down there to do that, but I wanted to see you and Jess first."

"You'll do no such thing. You'll stay here with me." She gestured to Luke, who'd taken a break.

Following Eleanor's gaze, Jayne watched him pull a bandanna out of his shorts pocket and wipe his brow, then take a swig of bottled water. Her attention riveted on his throat and she remembered with vivid clarity putting her mouth there.

"You can help me with my gardens, so Luke and Jess won't have to do that, too."

"It could take weeks to get a final verdict. I can't impose on you that long, Eleanor."

"At least wait until Jess gets back to make a decision."

She'd known this was going to be tricky before she came to town. Jess hadn't told his mother about Naomi's dislike of Jayne or the breach his wife's feelings had caused in Jayne's relationship with Jess. As far as Eleanor knew, Jayne had been too busy to visit Riverdale. Now, if she refused to stay, it wouldn't make sense to the older woman. Or to Luke. Jess had also kept Naomi's suspicions from him—at least he had in the past.

Oh, who was Jayne kidding? She wanted to stay.

She'd made the conscious decision to come to River-dale despite the consequences. "I guess I could do that."

"Then it's settled. You'll stay until at least next Saturday."

After petting the dog, which had jumped up on her lap, then setting the animal on the ground, Eleanor stood. "Now go get Luke. It's time for lunch."

"He'll eat with us?" The thought make her heart rate speed up.

Eleanor chuckled. "After he cleans up in the laundry room."

When Eleanor went into the house, Jayne rose and reluctantly made her way down the steps and through the flower beds toward the gazebo. Surrounded by their colorful blossoms and scent, with the sun on her face, Jayne experienced a sense of peace. She stopped and took a minute to steep herself in the rare emotion of contentment.

"I feel that way, too, when I'm here."

She hadn't realized she was a few feet away from Luke. "What are you talking about?"

"The gardens. They calm me. Your expression says they do the same to you."

Not wanting to encourage any connection with him, she turned her attention toward the gazebo. Unable to help herself, she ran her hand over the curved railing. "This is lovely. I especially like that the structure is cohesive with the house."

"I'm glad to have your approval." His tone was sarcastic.

Stiffening, she spoke curtly. "Eleanor said to tell you it's time for lunch."

He bit out, "I'm not fit for company."

"That's what I thought." She ignored his raised brow. "But she said you can clean up in the laundry room. You're sprung for the day, I guess." *I hope.*

"Maybe." He climbed down the ladder.

When Jayne turned to leave, he grabbed her by the arm and yanked her around. At the clasp of his strong fingers on her again, she startled. And damn it, she liked the feel of them. "How long are *you* hanging around?" he asked.

"Eleanor invited me to stay with her until Jess gets back."

"You can't do that."

"I can do whatever I want."

"Don't you care about how you've hurt everybody here?"

"Wh-what do you mean?"

"Stop playing innocent, like you did in New York. I never would have gotten you that contract with Madison Conglomerates if I'd known you'd slept with Jess." His expression turned hard. "And I *never* would have had a fling with you." His eyes narrowed. "It took me a while to figure out that was why you didn't want anyone back here to know we were involved."

"That had nothing to do with keeping our relationship quiet." Her voice rose with anger ignited by his accusation. "I like my privacy, is all. And I *never* slept with Jess."

"That's not what Naomi thinks. Hell, I still can't believe neither you nor Jess told me about her feelings."

"Because they weren't warranted."

"Or because Jess knew I wouldn't put in a good word with Granger Madison to get a junior associate from Prentice Architects a job on building those luxury condos."

"It was a job I did very well."

Crossing his arms over his bare chest, he glared at her. "Still, you ran away when there was a scandal at Prentice."

"I finished my part on the condos for Madison Conglomerates. I didn't like the direction Prentice Architects was taking, so I left when I got a better offer in California."

"Is that what you're telling yourself?"

"It's the truth."

"You ran, Jayne. Like you've been running all your life." He shook his head. "And you didn't even have the decency to talk to me about leaving. You didn't even say goodbye to me!"

Well, that was true. She'd never told him she'd taken a job in California because he would have—*could* have—kept her in New York. Luke was a fighter, had always been one, and she knew intuitively he would have fought to keep her with him. When things had calmed down, that fact made her incredibly sad. Yet she'd never contacted him again.

"In any case, Prentice Architects was exonerated. I read it in their follow-up correspondence."

"So you could have stayed."

"I told you that wasn't why I left."

His expression softened a bit. "Look, Jayne, I know that what happened in college to you and Jess affected you. But you shouldn't have run away at the threat of scandal."

Damn it, why had Jayne confided in him about the Cornell incident? "The two had nothing to do with each other."

From the porch they heard Eleanor call out, "Jayne, Luke, are you coming?"

Looking annoyed, Luke held up his hand. "If you stay in town, don't hurt Jess and his family again, or you'll answer to me."

"That sounds like a threat."

He stared down at her. His dark eyes had deepened to almost black and were intense. Angry. "If that's what's needed, then consider yourself threatened."

Since she'd made her mark in architecture, Jayne had often needed to deal with men on building sites. Early on, she'd learned how to be confident—or, when she wasn't, at least to look as if she was. She squared her shoulders and lifted her chin. "Back off, Luke. I'm not as easily intimidated as I was when I knew you in New York."

He made a sound of disgust. "I never knew you, lady. Never." With that, he stalked away.

She watched as he spoke quietly to Eleanor, unleashed the dog, picked her up and headed around the house. They made an incongruous picture—the big guy with the tiny puppy in his arms. Suddenly, Jayne wondered what had happened to him in the intervening years, if he'd ever married, had kids. And why on earth, after all this time, did the possibility of little boys with Luke's eyes or tiny girls with his smile make Jayne feel so bereft?

LUKE SWERVED his red truck into the driveway of his sister's house on Houghton Plot, got out and slammed the door. He tried not to think about Jayne Logan, but she'd gotten under his skin again, just like before, and it was a position he'd *never* put himself in with women since.

Little Karl came running out the door and toward him. "Uncle Luke!" he said as he flung himself at Luke. The boy was the spitting image of him, which always made him smile.

Right behind Karl was his brother, Kasey, tottering along on stocky little legs. His blond wispy hair was more like his dad's. Luke hefted the youngest up to his chest, then clasped Karl's shoulder.

Karl wrinkled his nose. "Eee-u, you stink."

"Been sweating my…butt off all morning." And since he'd made an excuse not to stay for lunch, he hadn't cleaned up either.

His older sister had followed her kids out and smiled warmly at him. Of all the girls, he resembled Belle the most. They both had dark hair and eyes, which explained Karl's resemblance to him.

"Hey, babe."

"You look mad. Certainly not at Miss Ellie."

He set his nephew down and let the dog out of the car. "Nah, she's got a guest who torqued me off."

Krystle nipped at the boys' feet and began to run around the front yard, making them giggle as they chased her. They loved playing with Maria's dog.

"Can you stay? Nick and Kenny are golfing. They're trying to spend some father/son time together." Belle had had one kid in her early twenties, then two more later on when she got bored with her job as a nurse and decided she wanted a bigger family.

"Yeah, my afternoon's clear."

Grinning, she kissed his cheek. "Go clean up, then I'll fix you lunch and we can chat after the boys go down for a nap."

"Sounds like a plan."

It was a good one. After a hot shower and a change into clothes he always left here and at his other sisters' houses, he made small talk with Belle during lunch and Luke paid attention to the kids. As always, they charmed him, even when Kasey smeared peanut butter over his face and then, when Luke laughed, covered his arms, too. Belle made him give the kid a bath, and then he put both boys down.

In a better mood now, he joined his sister out on the deck overlooking the wooded backyard. Never one to mince words, she said, "Okay, what happened, Luciano?" The only boy in the family, Luke was named after his dad.

He had to tread carefully here. For twelve years he'd kept his previous relationship with Jayne Logan secret from everyone, not because Jayne wanted it that way, but because initially he'd been embarrassed about how it had ended—a woman had actually dumped him! And then, when he'd gotten home and found out about Jayne and Jess, Luke had been humiliated at how she'd taken him in. "Do you remember Jayne Logan, Jess's friend?"

"The woman from college." Belle's eyes widened. "Oh, the one Naomi suspected Jess was involved with?"

Right after Luke came back to town, over a few late-night beers, Belle had told him about Naomi's suspicions concerning Jess and Jayne's relationship.

"Yeah, she's the one. She's in town and went looking for Jess. Since he's at Disney World, she hunted up Miss Ellie."

Belle cocked her head. "Miss Ellie loved Jayne. She came to Riverdale on vacations and even a summer or two and stayed with them." She frowned. "Much to Naomi's distress."

"Yeah, but Jayne abandoned Miss Ellie when she got rich and famous." She was very good at abandoning people.

"Why's she here now?"

"She's in trouble."

"What kind?"

"I didn't stick around to find out." In truth, he didn't want to know. He remembered his protective instincts where Jayne was concerned and he certainly didn't want to fall victim to them again.

Picking up her soft drink, Belle frowned. "Didn't you work with Jayne in New York?"

"Uh-huh. Briefly."

"Naomi said she made a name for herself in the architectural world in California and got caught up in the glamour and success there." Then Belle added gently, "You did too, Luke, when you became partners with Madison Conglomerates in New York."

"Yeah, but I learned my lesson. From what I've heard, she still feeds on fame."

Belle stood. "I'll be right back." She hustled off the porch and in no time returned with her laptop.

"What's that for?"

Luke had developed an aversion to the Internet. He kept all his business records on a computer, did e-mail and often ordered materials online, but he didn't surf in cyberspace anymore. He'd done all that when he'd first become successful. The Net was a connection to his previous life that he wanted to forget.

"*This* is a way to find out what trouble Jayne Logan's in."

Hmm, he guessed he could make this one exception. "Good thinking, Isabella, *mi amore*."

"Smarts run in the family, little brother. Now, isn't her first name spelled funny?"

ONE OF THE BEST things about Eleanor was that she took pleasure in small things, like this outing. For years,

Jayne had spun fantasies that if she ever had children, Eleanor would be a surrogate grandmother.

Jayne and Ben Scarborough, her college boyfriend of two years, had talked about having kids. Then he'd betrayed her, and that dream, with him at least, was dashed. Even when she'd met Luke, five years later, she was never able to completely trust him. When their relationship had begun to get serious, she'd fled.

"I'm paying, dear. I dragged you here." Eleanor was standing with Jayne in line at the Fox Theater, the only cinema in town, waiting to see the matinee of the new release of *The Little Mermaid*.

"You didn't drag me here. I'm happy to come. The last time I saw a Disney movie was when—" Jayne had to think "—I came with you and Jess to one in college."

"Ah, yes. He indulges my whims, too."

As they moved along, a warm breeze ruffled the tails of the pink shirt Jayne wore with jeans. "Jess sounded great on the phone when you let me talk to him."

"He was delighted that you're here."

Jayne smiled. "He threatened never to speak to me again if I left before he got back." She cleared her throat. "I didn't tell him what happened. I was afraid it would ruin his vacation."

"It would have. He loves you like a sister."

After Eleanor paid for their tickets, they went inside and crossed to the refreshment stand. "Smell that popcorn," Eleanor said. "I think I'll have some, with extra butter."

"You should be watching your cholesterol."

Unfortunately, Jayne recognized the deep masculine rumble from behind her. She turned to acknowledge Luke, but instead stood openmouthed when she took in the sight of him dressed in jeans and a green chamois shirt, holding a little boy of maybe two against the soft material that covered his chest. Clinging to his other hand was a child of about five, who looked exactly like him.

So he *was* married. With kids. For a moment, Jayne felt the world tip on its axis.

Eleanor said, "Hello, Luke. Oh, Kasey, you sweet boy. And Karl. Let me buy you a treat."

"Yes, Miss Ellie." The bigger one spoke first and the baby gave some version of it.

Luke raised his eyes to the ceiling. "I promised their mother I wouldn't let them have too much junk."

"How is Belle?" The name sounded familiar. Had he married an old girlfriend?

"Spending some time with Kenny while he's on his school break, so I'm babysitting."

Jayne frowned. "I wonder why it is that when men take care of their own kids, they call it babysitting?"

His expression turned blank, then he laughed.

Before he could respond, Karl said, "Uncle Luke, what's funny?"

Jayne flushed. "I thought…"

"Yeah, I can tell. They're my sister's kids. Karl, Kasey, meet Miss Logan." With a scowl, he added, "Is it still Miss?"

"Yes."

Karl greeted her, but Kasey buried his face in Luke's neck. And something inside of Jayne shifted. The gesture showed such spontaneous trust, was such a baby thing. Combined with what she'd been thinking earlier, about having her own kids, it had her…yearning.

"Would you like to sit with us, Luke?" Eleanor's expression was hopeful. "It would be such fun to see the boys' reactions to the movie."

Oh, no, Jayne thought, just as Luke said, "Great. We'd love to."

Inside the theater, the boys sat on opposite sides of Eleanor, and Jayne took the seat next to the littlest. But then Luke said, "Excuse me," and crawled over her to snatch Kasey out of the chair. He plunked down right next to her, with the baby on his lap. "There now, isn't this cozy?"

It was cramped and, this close, she could smell his aftershave—incredibly, the same one that he used to wear. The associations that brought back made her entire body respond. So she said, "I can move down so Kasey can have his own seat."

Luke gave her an are-you-stupid look. "He's too little to sit by himself."

And Kasey was apparently used to resting on his uncle's lap, because he cuddled in, stuck his finger in his mouth and began to watch the previews.

Jayne tried not to be distracted by the rhythmic stroking of Luke's big hand down the baby's wispy hair. She tried not to watch as he kissed the baby's head. But she began to experience an overwhelming sense of loss watching the gestures, being so close to Luke again. If she hadn't chickened out on her relationship with Luke, these could have been their kids. They could be married now and spending a lazy day as a family. When the movie began, she tried doubly hard to focus on Ariel and her adventure, until Karl leaned over Eleanor and whispered, "Uncle Luke, I gotta pee."

Luke said, "Great." He glanced at Eleanor, who held

a full bucket of popcorn on her lap, then lifted the baby and plopped him into Jayne's arms.

"What…what are you doing?"

"Taking Karl to the john." He stood, scooped up the boy, climbed over the back of his seat to an empty row and went out to the aisle.

Kasey looked up at her with wide blue eyes. She had no idea what to do with him. A smile spread across his adorable face, then he batted her cheeks with his chubby hands.

And she cooed, "Aren't you beautiful."

As if he'd gotten the answer he wanted, he nestled into *her* chest. He smelled like baby shampoo and powder, and Jayne reveled in the scent and the feel of his little body.

By the time Luke got back, Kasey was fast asleep, curled trustingly into her.

"I'll be damned. I wouldn't have guessed you had it in you."

Her either. "Just goes to show you how much you know."

"We'll see about that." He bit into a piece of licorice. "We'll just see about that."

CHAPTER THREE

LATE SATURDAY AFTERNOON, Jayne reached for the gardening shears to deadhead the snapdragons and pricked her thumb on the tip of a blade. "Ouch!"

By the gazebo, where he'd finished painting the first post blue, Luke snorted. Had she known he was going to show up so late in the day to put in an hour on the structure, she wouldn't have come out here. Now, he sat on one of the benches he'd built—she liked the way the legs of it angled—sipping a beer and making no effort to hide his study of her. "Watch out, Sleeping Beauty, or you'll go into a deep snooze."

Which Jayne wouldn't mind doing. Perhaps when she woke up, the nightmare of the investigation would be over. She'd checked with her lawyer this morning and there was no news.

What exactly does that mean, Michael? It's been three weeks.

These things take time. The architectural board is addressing it. You have to be patient.

What about the independent firm I hired to do its own analysis?

Nothing yet.

I can't believe this.

I'm sorry. I'll call you when I hear something.

"Hey, I'm talkin' to you."

She made a very unladylike noise. "Just so you don't get any ideas about playing Prince Charming." Again.

"No worries about that, babe. Once burned…"

Hmm. She'd always wondered how he'd handled her leaving, always wondered if it had left a hole inside him as it had, unexpectedly, in her. Probably not. He'd never tried to contact her. Most likely, she'd just bruised his ego.

There was no point in going there, though, so she nodded to the gazebo. "You know, you should paint the posts white."

He shook his head. "God, I hate it when people play Monday-morning quarterback."

His forceful tone reminded her of his reactions on the construction site in New York. She couldn't resist the temptation to jab him. "So you still think it's your way or the highway?"

"Yep."

"White would be a striking contrast."

"In case you didn't notice, I'm going for the fitting-in look with slate-blue."

"Too much fitting in is boring."

"Concentrate on those flowers, will you?"

Turning back to her plants, she picked up a trowel and began to loosen the dirt around the base of one. The rich loam of the earth was cold as it sifted through her fingers. She hadn't put on gloves because she liked the texture of it.

Luke sighed. "I wish Jess had made his plane connection in Atlanta this morning."

"He could still get back today."

"I know. Eleanor's keeping watch just in case."

Her head down, Jayne wiped her hands on the jeans she'd cut off to work out here. She'd borrowed some old work shoes she'd found in Eleanor's downstairs closet. "I love how close Eleanor and Jess are."

Before he could comment, someone called out, "There she is!"

At the sound of the voice, Jayne glanced up and saw Jess standing at the base of the porch steps. He looked so good, so safe and unbreakable, that she threw the shovel to the ground, stood and ran toward him. Jess met her halfway, picked her up and whirled her around. When he stopped, one arm banded her around her waist and his other hand went to her head to bring it to his chest. Jayne was so grateful for the embrace she wanted to cry. But she hadn't shed one tear since college and had vowed, with this very man during the ordeal at Cornell they'd shared, that she'd never cry again.

Luke watched the reunion. Jess held Jayne as if he'd found gold, and she clung to him like they'd been lovers separated for years. And goddamn it, sparks of jealousy shot through him and he hated feeling that way about his best friend.

Then he caught sight of Naomi. The kids must be in the house, but Jess's wife had accompanied him back here and was standing behind him. Her face was pale, despite her tan, and her brow was furrowed.

As Luke witnessed the reunion between the two college friends and Naomi's devastated expression, he cursed Jayne Logan's return to Riverdale. Especially after he'd found out on his sister's computer that the woman had botched her last job and might be permanently available to wreak more havoc in Jess's life.

WHEN JAYNE OPENED her eyes and saw Naomi staring at her and Jess as if they were embracing naked, she immediately drew back. Damn it, why had she been so spontaneous in greeting Jess? And what had he been thinking? She looked at him and saw that he *wasn't* thinking. Tears clouded his warm hazel eyes. Naomi obviously caught on to her husband's sentimentality, because she paled. Jayne tried to pull away from Jess completely, but he slid his arm around her and held her close to his side.

Jayne was the one to acknowledge the other woman. "Hi, Naomi."

"Jayne."

Spinning around, Jess got a glimpse of his wife. "I thought you were in the house."

"Obviously. I'm going to take the girls home." Naomi added brusquely, "They'll be getting cranky."

Jess frowned. "But I want Jaynie to see them." When Naomi simply stared at him, he added, "We agreed on that."

"*Jaynie* can do that tomorrow." She glanced behind them. "Hey, Luke."

Luke crossed to the group but went straight to Naomi, hugged her and whispered something into her ear. Then he turned to Jess. "Hey, buddy."

"Man, hi. I missed you."

"You've only been gone two weeks."

Jess let go of Jayne to give Luke a quick hug. "But I've gotten used to you being around."

Luke smiled. "I missed you, too."

Grabbing Jayne's hand, Jess tugged her forward. "I take it you got reacquainted with our girl."

"Yeah." After glaring at her, Luke pivoted. Naomi

had already started to walk away. "Wait up, Nay, I want to see the girls."

She glanced at her husband, then at Luke. "Maybe you can give us a lift home. Goodbye, Jayne. Jess, I'll see you…whenever."

When the two of them disappeared into the house, Jayne faced Jess. "Why don't you go with Naomi and we can catch up tomorrow? She's not happy about you staying with me."

"Hush, it's the same old, same old." His features took on a hard edge. "And damn her for it. We had an agreement six years ago."

Again, he took Jayne's hand and they walked to Luke's gazebo. Inside, the scents of paint and fresh wood enveloped her; they made her think about working on a construction site. Once they were sitting on a curved bench, she told him about the collapse of the walkway in the Coulter Gallery.

"I'm so sorry, Jaynie."

She swallowed hard. "Sometimes I still can't believe it."

"Why didn't you call me when it happened? This is the kind of emergency we agreed to contact each other about."

"I didn't want to burden you."

"Tell me about the collapse."

Because he'd been an architectural student, he understood the logistics. "You know the walkway circles the second floor of the gallery."

"I saw pictures on the Internet. It's beautiful."

"It was. Other galleries have done the same thing, so it wasn't that risky. But something went wrong, and a portion of it just…fell."

"How much?"

"Maybe twenty-five feet. Thankfully it was at night, so no one was hurt. I don't know what I would have done if…" She shivered and Jess squeezed her hand.

"Don't think about that."

"You're right. There's enough to worry about." She told him the staggering cost of the damage. She had insurance, thank the Lord, but her reputation could be in tatters if she was somehow found at fault—or even if she wasn't. Bad press could ruin an architectural firm. She might not even keep the jobs already contracted.

When she finished with the details, Jess sighed deeply. "It is what it is. If you made a mistake, which I'm not saying you did, there are ways to deal with it." He added soberly, "You can do anything you have to, honey, you know that. Just like the Snyder incident."

Al Snyder had been their third-year design teacher at Cornell. He'd based a major portion of the grade for the semester on a group project. Though Jayne hated being evaluated on others' efforts, she'd felt comfortable that time because the members of her group were Jess and their two housemates—Ben, her boyfriend of two years, and Sally, a close girlfriend.

At least Jayne had thought they were her friends, until their part of the project came under scrutiny. When it was discovered they'd cut corners by falsifying data, Ben and Sally blamed it on Jess and Jayne. Jayne ended her relationship with Ben, but her confidence had been shaken. If he could betray her so badly, had he ever really cared about her? Had she ever been enough for him?

That event had touched off Naomi's animosity. Jess had called Naomi, his fiancée at the time, to tell her what had happened. Without informing him of her plans, Naomi had driven up to Ithaca to comfort him.

Instead, she found him, literally, in bed with Jayne. Jess was bare chested and in boxers; Jayne wore a skimpy tank top and short pajama bottoms, so the scenario was incriminating. But it was totally innocent—they'd both been devastated after the betrayal of their housemates and Jayne had gone to Jess's room for comfort. Naomi never believed it, though. And in subsequent years, she'd found more and more reason to be jealous of any time her husband spent with Jayne.

Hurt all over again by her recollection of the devastating event, Jayne shook off the memory. "I know I can get through it. But I never thought I'd have such a monumental thing to deal with again. And I hated that the first one caused you to leave school."

"It wasn't the only reason I left, Jaynie."

"I know it wasn't. You weren't really happy at Cornell and couldn't wait to get back to Riverdale. If it hadn't been for my dad bringing in a team of New York lawyers, I would have left, too."

By the end of the year, both she and Jess had been exonerated—and the college had dropped the whole matter, punishing no one—but kind, sweet Jess's heart wasn't in architecture like hers was. He'd come home to Riverdale, finished a four-year degree at a local college in social work and went into community service. He'd been ecstatic when, ten years ago, he'd been appointed head of Harmony Housing, which built low-income housing projects subsidized by the government and involving several volunteer groups.

"Anyway, there's nothing you can do but wait, so you'll do it here."

"That's what your mother said."

"She's a smart woman."

"Luke Corelli doesn't feel the way you do."

Jess shook his head. "He's way overprotective."

"Because he knows how Naomi feels about me and you?"

"You know about that?"

"Luke made a point of bringing it up."

"Maybe that's why he's protective, but other things have happened to him."

Jayne didn't ask what. She'd decided last night that the less she knew about Luke's life, the better.

"I'm sorry Naomi still misunderstands our relationship."

"Me, too. I know intellectually it's because her father and brother cheated on their spouses, and I try to understand that, but I resent her for grouping me in with all of them. Hell, we've been married for seventeen years."

"You can avoid feeding her fears, Jess, like we decided to do six years ago."

Again his features hardened and his hazel eyes sharpened. "That's not going to happen. I stopped seeing you then to appease her. It worked. No fights, nothing. I told her, though, if you ever needed me, I was going to be there for you. Now, she's reneging on her part when I kept my promise. I haven't put my foot down about anything else, but I won't let you go through this alone."

"I…"

"Damn it, Jayne. It infuriates me that we never gave her reason to be jealous and I still had to end my relationship with you."

"I know."

"Please say you'll stay."

She wanted to, badly. And she was weakening.

"Well, it might be a good idea to put off working on those new projects until I'm sure the firm will keep them. What could I *do* here?"

Jess chuckled. "I know just the thing."

LUKE SAT on Jess's front porch and watched dusk fall on Riverdale. He was so glad to be back in town, he sometimes wondered why he'd ever left in the early nineties.

Fame and fortune, Timmy had said. *We'll make millions in the building boom in Dubai. Just think, no more depending on family. No more scrimping or dilapidated cars.*

Luke hadn't minded depending on his family, but the fact that there was never enough money to go around always bothered him. And he'd lost his chance at an athletic scholarship when he blew his knee out playing football, so he'd thrown caution to the winds and gone overseas with Timmy. It had been the worst decision of his life, because they had indeed made money, and it destroyed his friend.

"Want something?" Naomi stood behind the screen leading to the kitchen.

Luke held up his beer. "Already got it." When she came out, he studied the slim blonde with sad blue eyes. "You look as tired as the girls. I should leave."

"No, don't." She dropped down beside him on a padded porch chair. "I won't sleep until Jess gets back."

"Will you fight?"

"Who knows? Now that Jayne Logan is back in our lives, anything could happen."

"This is so unlike Jess. I can't figure it out."

Naomi shook her head. "Join the club." Her voice

trembled. "I can't believe he's doing this to me again. It was horrible when he went to California to see her, or when she visited here and they spent time together. But I thought his contact with her was over."

"He swears there's nothing between them, Nay. That they never had an affair."

"I'm so sick of that argument. Even if it never got physical—which I find hard to believe, especially after seeing her again, seeing how pretty she is—the emotional connection between them is enough of a betrayal." She shook her head. "They're so close, Luke."

"I could tell."

"You don't like her much, do you?"

He had a blinding flash of tangled sheets, sweaty bodies, and Jayne clinging to him as he drove into her. "Uh, no."

"Why?"

"For one, I know the part she's played in the trouble between you and Jess. Second, I met women like her in my old life." He thought of tall, slender and very sophisticated Elizabeth Madison, whom he thought he was going to marry. "They aren't known for their loyalty. She also reminds me of *me* when I was working in that world."

"You weren't so bad."

"Thanks, sweetie. But I was."

"Is this about Timmy again?"

"I don't want to talk about Timmy. In any case, Jess should respect your wishes, Nay."

Slowly, she ran her finger around the top of the glass. "To be fair, he's done that for six years."

"What do you mean?"

Looking up at him, she asked, "He didn't tell you why he hasn't seen her in all that time?"

"No. I thought he just realized the cost was too high."

"He didn't go into specifics?"

Luke shook his head. He'd never wanted to talk about Jayne with Jess, because of what he'd found out when he got back to Riverdale, and because of what had occurred between the two of them in New York.

"Six years ago, she offered him a job as manager of her firm—one with a big salary. When he considered taking it, I freaked out. Things got so bad between us that I threatened to leave him, so he turned the offer down and finally promised me he wouldn't see her anymore."

"I didn't know that. I thought they just drifted apart. Or she got too rich and famous to bother with him anymore."

"Yeah, well, it was tough all around. My father was in rehab, and his women friends made no bones about visiting him there. My brother was mired in his own marital problems and I was a wreck. So Jess agreed not to see Jayne and I agreed to get some counseling. Except…" She bit her lip. "He did talk to her periodically, but even that dwindled. The only caveat was he told her—and me—that if she ever needed him, he'd be there for her. I, um, agreed to that."

Damn it to hell. Luke was pissed he hadn't known all this. They'd kept *everything* from him.

"Things were so good without the shadow of Jayne Logan in our lives. Why did she have to come back now?"

"She's in trouble."

"I figured it had to be something like that. What happened?"

"The walkway of a gallery she designed collapsed.

There's an investigation going on that she can't be part of, so she came here. For emotional support."

"Damn. I thought maybe she'd have to get back to her glamorous life." Naomi shook her head, sending the bob of her hair swirling. "Is she guilty?"

"Most likely. People cut corners all the time."

"You and Jess don't at Harmony Housing."

"No, we don't." But Luke had done his share of compromising in his other life and learned his lesson.

Naomi rubbed her temples. "Let's change the subject. This is giving me a headache. How's work?"

"Good. I like contracting for Harmony Housing."

Though he used to take on other projects, Luke now worked exclusively for his best friend's organization because they'd just gotten approval for twenty units.

Naomi shook her head and sipped her glass of wine. "You work too cheaply for Harmony."

"Nah." He smiled. "The foundation's done for the first house. We start framing on Monday."

"Jess loves working with you, Luke."

"I feel the same way. As an added bonus, I can find some jobs for Corrine's husband."

"Belle said they're having a hard time making ends meet."

"I wouldn't know. When I asked Corky, she told me to mind my own business." He shook his head. "Something's going on with her and Cal, I think, but none of the girls know what. Corky can be pretty private. Probably comes with being the oldest."

"Poor Luke, still getting bossed around by his four big sisters."

He chuckled.

The crickets chirped in the yard and they listened to

them for a while in companionable silence. Then Naomi asked, "How's Erica?"

"Not seeing her anymore. I'm dating Elise Jenkins." He was quiet. "Erica wanted a commitment."

"Luke, you're thirty-eight years old. You should be thinking about settling down."

"I tried. Didn't work out."

"Because you picked somebody from your other world to get engaged to."

"I'm doing okay for now, Nay."

"You want kids."

"Yeah, I do. But I content myself with yours and my sisters' to spoil."

"The Pied Piper of Riverdale."

"Want me to go over to Eleanor's and lure Jess home?"

"The very fact that you'd have to do that makes me sick. No, he'll come when he's ready."

Reaching over, Luke took her hand. "It'll be okay."

"Sure."

Too bad neither one of them believed his reassurance.

CHAPTER FOUR

LUKE STOOD OVER the foundation of the new Harmony Housing and felt a sense of anticipation, as he always did at the beginning of a construction project. He savored the smell of newly poured concrete for the basement. When the outer shell took shape—the joists and girders, the frame and the plywood, and finally the roof—he experienced a father's pride for what he'd lovingly created. He'd never told anybody about his sense of connection with the buildings he helped put up, not even Timmy or, now, Jess.

"Looking good, isn't it?" His brother-in-law Cal Sorvino had come up to him. Cal appeared tired this morning, and Luke noticed again how much weight the man had gained.

"Yeah." Luke tipped back his hard hat, feeling the sweat on his scalp. April had turned into no-coat weather. "Was it okay helping out with the foundation?"

Cal ducked his head, embarrassed. "Yeah, sure. We need the money, with Louie going to college next year."

Luke bit back his opinion. Cal was an electrician and good at what he did, but with the economy not doing well, there weren't a ton of jobs in his field, especially in the winter. Still, he should be making ends meet, but he wasn't good at managing his money. Luke's sister

Corky did her best—she worked full-time as a paralegal—but for as long as Luke could remember, they'd had financial problems. And unbeknownst to Corky, Luke gave Cal money periodically. "You're industrious, Cal, taking on construction."

"Not all of us have stashes in the bank."

Stiffening, Luke glanced away. He'd made more money than he'd ever need in those years overseas, then again when he returned to the U.S. and joined Madison Conglomerates. The cash had flowed freely, but so had the booze and cocaine. He'd been able to handle the latter, but Timmy hadn't.

Cal said, "I see you hired on Mick O'Malley."

"Yeah." Luke's gaze strayed to Timmy's older brother. Unlike Cal, Mick was thin and his shoulders were perennially hunched. "He's strapped, too."

"He hates your guts."

"He's got a reason."

"No, he doesn't. Timmy's drug use wasn't your fault."

Of course it was. Luke had been busy himself, trying to get ahead, and then Jayne Logan had entered his life and he'd got wrapped up in her, spent as much time with her as she'd allowed. If he hadn't been so enthralled with her, maybe Timmy…

Luke was distracted from the thought when Jess's Jeep pulled up to the site. He wondered how things had gone over the weekend with Naomi. Jess climbed out of the driver's side, wearing an outfit similar to Luke's—jeans, work boots and a navy-blue T-shirt that read Live in Harmony.

Then the passenger door opened and Jayne slid out of that side. What the *hell* was Jess doing bringing her to the site? She wore jeans, too, and a Harmony T-shirt that fit her…nicely. A blinding burst of lust came out of nowhere and slammed into Luke as he remembered exploring every single inch of her.

"Hey, guys." Jess looked as if he hadn't gotten much sleep, but he managed a smile.

"Jess." Luke tipped his hard hat to Jayne. "Hi. What brings you here?"

Jayne glanced at Jess. "I came to see Jess's project. I've never been to a Harmony Housing site." When Luke didn't respond, she asked, "You head the construction, right?"

Luke nodded to his truck, where *Corelli Contracting* was scrawled across the door. "Yeah."

Jess grinned. "He runs the show, is what he does. Gives me time for paperwork and supervision."

"You've hunted up a bricklayer and hammered a few nails yourself," Luke said.

"Not like you." Jess leaned closer to Jayne. "Luke usually works alongside whoever he hires."

"A real man's man."

"Yep," Jess said, his tone full of pride. Apparently he'd missed the sarcasm of her quip.

"Come on, Jaynie." Jess tugged on her arm. "Let me show you the plans for this set of houses. We're building twenty-five, and ten of them are in this tract."

Sadness flitted across Jayne's face. Briefly, Luke wondered what it would be like to be kept from doing the job you loved. He felt a stab of guilt for not having more sympathy for her, especially when he recalled how vulnerable she had been when he'd first met her in New York.

They walked away and Luke stared after them, mesmerized by the gentle sway of Jayne's hips until he heard a low whistle behind him. Pivoting, he found one of the framers, a young man in his twenties, tracking his gaze. "Andy, I'd watch that if I were you. Sexual harassment is illegal these days."

Andy snorted. "I saw you undressin' her with your eyes, boss."

Shit. He turned and headed over to a nearby truck, where workers were unloading steel girders. Time for some physical labor if his attraction to Jayne Logan was that easy to spot.

SEATED IN Jess's trailer at a table by the window, Jayne pored over the plans for the low-income units Harmony Housing was building. She always did this on her own projects—checked the specs, the slopes and the dimensions like a mother carefully going over her child's weight, height and girth. What on earth would Jayne do if she lost her babies and couldn't design buildings anymore? If the architectural board found gross negligence? Or just plain stupidity?

Jess put his hands on her shoulders. "You'll get to do it again, Jaynie."

"You always could read my mind."

He dropped down next to her. "It's written all over your face." An encouraging smile. "I can help you wait this out."

"I'm still not sure…"

"Don't you want to be part of Harmony Housing? The volunteers always need help."

Jayne ran her fingers over the blue-lined drawings. "Truthfully, I want to. But it's not the best thing for you."

"Can we please get off that?"

"No. Think of how Naomi would react if I was working with you every day."

He drew in an exasperated breath. "Do you have any idea what it's like when the person you love most in the world thinks you're a cheater? That she groups me with the men in her family? It hurts like hell."

Jayne remembered loving Ben so much. When he betrayed her, she thought she'd die. She'd truly believed he was the man for her, and that he meant it when he said he loved her and they'd be together forever. His betrayal had ultimately kept her from throwing herself into a relationship with Luke. At least she hadn't invested too much in him.

"I only know how bad it felt when Ben turned on me." Jayne covered his hand with hers. "It's different when you're married."

"Stay, Jaynie. At least until you find out what's going on with your career." She hesitated, and he added, "Can I please have my way for a change?"

When she didn't answer, Jess stood and drew her into a hug. For a minute she let his easy affection comfort her. She wanted to stay here with him. And she needed something to do if she was to delay new projects until the architectural board decided. "All right. I'll work on your houses until the board makes its decision."

The door to the trailer opened. Jayne looked over to find Luke in the entrance. His eyes narrowed, and she realized the way she and Jess were standing could be misconstrued.

"Isn't this cozy? You said nothing was going on between you two."

Pulling back, Jess took her hand and brought her closer to Luke. "Nothing is. Like you mean, anyway. Actually, we were sealing the deal."

"What deal?"

"Jayne's agreed to work at Harmony Housing until she goes back to California."

She thought Luke was going to pop a blood vessel. "Why? So she can screw up more buildings?"

JAYNE SHOOK HER HEAD and gave Luke a look that made him feel like he'd just kicked a puppy. "I'm going to wander around the site, Jess." Her voice was hoarse. Hurt. Without saying a word to Luke, she went out the still-open door. Jess rounded on Luke.

"That was cruel."

"Maybe, but I don't care about her feelings."

His friend's face reddened. "How can you say that?"

Because she didn't care about mine when she left me high and dry. "Because you need to hear the truth, even if you don't want to. That woman isn't good for you, and having her in town, let alone at the site, is a very bad idea."

Jess's features were stern and very un-Jess-like. "I don't want to talk to you about Jayne." Jess cocked his head. "You didn't want to talk about her, either, when you came back to town. I always wondered why, since you worked with her for almost a year."

Luke just stared at Jess. "That was the worst time in my life."

"Because of Timmy."

Luke didn't respond.

"All right. You're entitled to your feelings. But you're not entitled to hurt Jayne. What were you thinking, saying something like that to her? Do you have any idea how fragile she is now?"

Fragile would be the last word he'd apply to the current Jayne Logan, though that look she'd given him had pierced even *his* hardened heart. "Because of the building collapse?"

"For one thing. But Luke, she doesn't have family like we do to support her. And she's had some pretty big blows in life to deal with alone." He scowled. "How did you know about the Coulter Gallery collapse, anyway?"

"Isabella looked her up on the Internet."

"So you'd have ammunition against Jayne." Wearily, Jess sank behind his desk.

After a moment, Luke dropped into the chair in front of it. "Listen, I'm just worried about Naomi."

Jess shook his head. "This is all wearing so thin. You know what I've been thinking about? When you have to keep doing penance for a sin you didn't commit, you start wondering if you might as well just do it."

Luke felt his blood pressure rise. The thought of Jayne and Jess together, like that, like Luke had been with her, enraged him. Damn it, he *never* got jealous. "Oh, great, she's back in town only a few days and she's got you thinking about screwing her."

Jess didn't say anything. Often his best weapon was silence.

"Tell me the truth now." Luke was thinking about how pretty Jayne was, how passionate she'd been in his arms, how great she'd always made him feel in bed. "In the cold light of day. What if you could have more? Have Jayne in your life permanently?"

"You know, maybe if people would *let* me have her in my life, without insisting it was going to turn into something sexual, then you'd see nothing has happened—or ever will happen." He stood. "I'm tired of rehashing this. I'm going out to find her. I hope she hasn't left the site."

Guilt, deep and heavy, had Luke standing, too. And something else. Residual feelings for Jayne he was forced to acknowledge. Damn! He could understand the white-hot attraction that kept coming back, but how *could* he still care about her after all this time, after how she'd left him? "No, let me go find her. I'll apologize."

Jess watched him with eyes full of real pain. Luke cursed himself for hurting his friend. Maybe some soul baring was in order. "If it helps any, she reminds me of who I used to be, Jessie. Who I was when I knew her in New York."

"You say that as if she's committed a crime by choosing the life she has."

"I hate her world."

"I think she does, too. You have more in common than you think."

Luke frowned.

"Be careful with her, Luke. I mean it."

Outside, the air had gotten even warmer, or maybe it was being on the hot seat that made Luke sweat. He scanned the area and didn't see Jayne anywhere. Oh, man, he hoped she hadn't left. Sometimes Luke could kick himself for his tendency to bully, to orchestrate things, to fix them in a way he thought they should be fixed. In times of stress, he couldn't seem to control that fault. He crossed to the foundation and was relieved to find her in the basement, inspecting the work that had been done.

Seeing her down there catapulted him into the past. One Saturday morning, when the crews had been off and the site where Madison Conglomerates was building the condos was empty, he and Jayne had been walking around the perimeter, and he'd gone down into the foundation. She'd followed him down the ladder and jumped on his back, her legs banding around him. It was about three months into their relationship and she'd gotten more playful by then, her caution because of asshole Ben Scarborough diminishing. Luke had given her a piggyback ride for a few feet. Then he stopped, pivoted suddenly and anchored her against the cinder blocks. She'd encouraged him, and he'd kissed her senseless. He had her shirt open before he realized where they were. They giggled all the way back to her father's corporate apartment, where she was staying, and they made playful love the rest of the morning.

After seeing her and Jess together this morning, after hearing Jess talk about committing a sin, Luke realized he wanted to murder anybody who got to touch her. Including his best friend. What exactly did that say about him?

No matter, he thought, picking up a hard hat. He had to go do his least favorite thing—eat some crow.

LUKE'S WORDS PLAGUED Jayne.

Why? So she can screw up more buildings?

Against her will, she remembered how he used to be her champion: *You were right to stand up to the building inspector… Good for you, insisting the plumber change what he'd done wrong… Man, you are so smart about these plans. Nobody else saw what you did.*

Now he thought she was a screwup.

On top of that, Luke's pithy comment in the trailer had given her a preview of what she'd face if she was guilty…or maybe even if she wasn't. Reputation was everything in the architectural world. When she started to panic at the thought of losing the most important thing in her life, the *only* thing in her life, she took deep breaths and tried to concentrate on the building around her. But Luke's accusation hammered inside her head and she felt ill.

From the corner of her eye, she saw someone climbing down the ladder. Expecting Jess, Jayne was surprised to see Luke. He descended gracefully for such a big man. She'd always loved that about him—his agility, his gentleness for someone his size. When she began to remember what that meant in bed, she adjusted her hard hat over her eyes to cover her expression as he strode toward her. She had to stand up to him, but he'd taken the wind out of her sails earlier—which hadn't been hard, because her self-confidence now was only a whisper of a breeze. Still, she steeled herself as he reached her.

"I'm sorry I said that. It was mean and uncalled-for."

She hadn't expected an apology, knew he hated to make them, and waited to hear what he'd say next.

"I was out of line, but what are you thinking to even consider working with Harmony Housing? I can't imagine what Naomi will do when she finds out."

Jayne shook her head. "I can see how sorry you are."

"I'm not very good at apologizing." He rolled his eyes. "I don't do it very often."

"I remember."

"I'm overprotective of Jess."

She looked away. "My coming to Riverdale was a mistake."

"Isn't there somebody in California you could go to?"

Keeping her gaze averted, she shook her head.

"Why, Jayne?" His tone had softened, making her go mushy inside. "Why didn't you ever find anybody out there to share your life with?"

"I won't talk about that with you."

"Why not?"

Because, once she'd left Luke and dated other guys, she'd realized if she couldn't make it with him, she probably couldn't make it with anyone else. And after two failed relationships, she'd thrown herself into her work and only dated casually.

He lifted a hand, dropped it in a helpless gesture. "Never mind. I don't want to know about you and other men, anyway. Do what you want about staying. Especially if you have nowhere else to go."

"Before Jess convinced me to stay, I was planning to go to my condo in Florida and work on new projects. Perhaps that was a good idea after all."

"And be alone while the architectural board is making a decision?"

"I'm used to being alone."

"I can't fathom that."

"Because you've always had your family and friends to depend on. You have no idea how lucky you are."

"I'm sorry about that, Jayne." He pulled off his hard hat to reveal spiky, wet hair. "I always hated how your family treated you."

She lifted her chin. "Yes, well. None of that matters." To change the subject, she pointed to the foundation. "I see you used concrete instead of cinder blocks. It's not that popular in California."

He tracked her gaze. "It sets faster, so we can get on with the house quicker." He was silent a moment.

"Look, stay in town if you want, but try to stay out of my way on the site, and I'll do the same with you."

She eyed him carefully, waiting for the other shoe to drop.

It did. "And try not to cause trouble between Naomi and Jess." He shook his head. "I hope you both know what you're doing." He started toward the ladder without giving her a chance to respond.

As she watched him walk away, she wondered how she was going to be able to avoid Luke on the site. Given the current state of her affairs, she wasn't sure she had the strength to take him on, too.

THAT AFTERNOON, Luke rounded the corner of the trailer and stopped short. Jayne stood near the flatbed truck that delivered the lumber, hefting one end of several two-by-fours bound together, while someone else picked up the wood in the truck. The load weighed way more than she could handle. Her face was flushed; sweat beaded on it. He strode over to her to shore up the beams.

"What do you think you're doing?" she asked hotly as he took the brunt of the weight by standing in front of her and grabbing the long two-by-fours.

"I could ask you the same thing." He waited until the lumber was set on the ground and the man was off the truck, then turned to the foreman of his general contracting crew, who also oversaw the volunteer work. "Ranaletti, why'd you let her haul this stuff? It weighs a ton."

"She insisted." Ranaletti was a good guy and seemed amused. "I thought she'd topple over at first lift. But she didn't."

In Luke's peripheral view, he saw Jayne fume. She

bent down, hoisted up the wood and nodded to the guy at the other end. "Let me help you get this over to the foundation, John." She glared at Luke. "Then I can come back and fight with *you*."

"I said I'd carry it." Not only did her overexertion piss him off, he also wasn't used to people questioning him on the site.

"Like hell. I was doing just fine until you rushed here on your white horse."

He stared her down; she moved in closer and nudged him out of the way with her shoulder. "I mean it, Luke."

Damn it. Let her pull a muscle. Maybe an injury would keep her out of the way. He stepped back.

Though her biceps strained, she carried the lumber—backward no less—over to the foundation. Yanking off her hard hat, she stalked back to him. Those violet eyes looked like purple flame and her damp hair gleamed in the sun. Her face was beet-red. Appealingly, Luke thought incongruously, as she was ready to ream him out. "Don't you *ever* do that again."

"Excuse me? I'll run this site however I choose. I *am* the contractor."

"Damn you, you said you'd stay out of my way. Or did you just mean I should stay out of yours?"

Actually, he had.

"Oh, God, you did." She stood straight and threw back her shoulders. "Don't interfere with what I'm doing." Her expression was haughty and, despite her somewhat be-draggled appearance, she seemed like royalty. "In case you didn't notice, I carried that just fine."

He'd noticed. "You're stronger than you used to be. So what?"

"FYI, I can bench-press my own weight and I run two miles every day. I'm in great shape."

Because he couldn't disagree with the proof of her buff body, and because curiosity got the better of him, he asked, "How come?"

"So," she said, again like queen chiding her subject, "I don't have to deal with chauvinists like you pushing *the little lady* out of the way." She turned and walked back to the truck.

"Ooo-ee," Ranaletti said, "she sure told you, boss."

"The bitch." This from Hank Herman, a framer who had no tact and never dealt well with women in construction.

"Man, how long is she going to be here?" Juan Gomez asked. He was a peacemaker and one of Luke's favorite workers.

Luke faced his crew. They shouldn't be letting loose with nasty comments, but since he'd just made an ass out of himself as an example, he didn't correct them.

Damn it, how the hell was he going to keep his head on straight and run the site with this woman from his past in his way? Especially since all he really wanted to do was jump her bones?

ONCE AGAIN, Jayne sat in the trailer late that afternoon, taking a break from physical labor. She'd been glad to get away from Luke, who was watching her like a hawk. On the desk, she noticed a picture of Jess, Luke and Timmy, probably from high school, as they were all wearing football jerseys.

"Jess, where's Timmy?"

Jess's hand froze on the cell phone he was about to use. "Timmy?"

"Yeah, I haven't heard you or Luke talk about him much."

"We don't." He perched on the edge of the desk.

"Why?"

"I…" His phone rang. Jess seemed relieved when he said, "Gotta take this. Why don't you check out the plans more closely? See if there's anything that doesn't look up to speed to you."

Jess answered the call. After a moment, he rose, went to the file cabinet and got out a folder. Before today, she'd had no idea how complicated his job was. He'd dealt with paperwork for the funding all morning, and now he was trying to set up delivery schedules for floor tile.

Jayne rolled out the blueprints and began to study them. It was a while before he ended the call and crossed to her. Hunching his shoulders back and forth to let out the tension, she guessed, he said, "How do they look?"

"I, um, think you could do more for the home owners with a few changes." She traced a line in the kitchen drawing. "If you moved this wall, you'd still have plenty of space in the dinette, and you could put in a small laundry room over here."

Jess examined the blueprints, as he used to in college before he quit. "Actually, I thought about that early on. But we were working with a new architect, and he and I didn't agree on a lot of things." Again he scrutinized the plans. "It wouldn't cost much more than the wiring and some additional lumber." Smiling at Jayne, he reached over to his desk, got a yellow pad and pencil, and handed them to her. "Sketch that out and note anything in the rest of the house you think could be improved without spending too much more money.

There's still time for floor-plan changes at this stage. I'll go over it with Luke before we shut down for the day."

Her heart started to beat fast. God, she so wanted to work on a building design again. "You sure?"

"Yep."

"Luke won't like it."

"He'll be okay with it. He had his own run-in with the architect. We ended up not hiring him back."

Still, she doubted Luke would be amenable to her suggestions. Too bad. She was furious at his earlier behavior.

After Jess left, Jayne spent a blissful hour looking over the rest of the plans, making notes for inexpensive improvements. When she finished, there were a lot of scribbles on the legal pad. And she'd loved every second of it. The problem was, as she'd worked, a gaping hole had formed in her heart, reminding her she could lose her license and never be able to do this again.

Standing, she stretched her back, which hurt from sitting down too long. Or maybe from lifting the lumber. She walked to the door of the trailer, which Jess had left open for the warm air to drift in, and scanned the site. They'd made a lot of progress today, getting up some of the outer shell and steel joists. This was one of her favorite times in construction—seeing the frame of the building take shape. Technically, architects didn't need to be on the site unless there was a problem. But learning from the actual construction—what worked, what didn't work, how she could improve things—had helped her succeed in her field. She just had to get past the barrier of contractors who wondered why she was there.

Off to the side, she caught sight of Jess and Luke

talking. Unable to see Jess's face, she unfortunately got a good glimpse of Luke's. His features were set in a stern frown, and there was heat in his eyes. She remembered another kind of heat there—sometimes when he just looked at her, but always when he touched her, always when he drove into her with a passion he couldn't harness. Damn it, she couldn't afford to have these kinds of thoughts about him.

He gestured and scrubbed a hand over his jaw. Then he glanced at the trailer and, when he saw her, he scowled.

Uh-oh.

He and Jess came over to the trailer.

When they reached her, Jess gave her a smile, but it was weak. "I was just telling Luke I asked you to look at the house plans, that you had some suggestions."

"He doesn't seem too happy about it."

Luke snapped, "I'm here, you two, in case you haven't noticed. No need to talk about me in the third person."

"Oh, I noticed. What have I done now?" She played innocent, but she knew very well what irked him.

"Have you any idea what a pain in the ass it is to change interior plans at the eleventh hour because of an architect's whim?"

She bristled. "Whim? Give me a break. Changes need to be made in all buildings as they go up."

"At the risk of setting a precedent and refereeing you two on this site, neither of us was satisfied with Anderson's drawings, Luke."

"They were good enough."

Jayne couldn't help but comment. "I don't think so."

"Yeah, like what?"

"Come on in," Jess said in a conciliatory tone. "Have a Coke and look at what she's got."

As they stepped inside, Jayne's stomach tightened. Suddenly, she wished she hadn't made so many suggestions. He'd always hated interference.

Jayne crossed to the plans and picked up the yellow pad. She handed it to Luke.

He scanned the front page, then the second. Then he looked up. "You gotta be kidding me."

HARRY'S BAR in the center of town was frequented mostly by laborers: builders, plumbers, electricians, construction workers and city maintenance people. Luke liked its lack of pretentiousness and—okay, he'd admit it—the male atmosphere of the place. Women rarely darkened its doorway and he appreciated the camaraderie and talk of work, as well as the sports blaring from the three overhead sets. The place always smelled of fresh beer and the peanut shells strewn on the floor.

Snagging a stool at the end of the scarred oak bar, he ordered a Coors. Right about now, he could use a double Manhattan. Though he used to favor the drink in his old life, he stayed away from it these days. As he sipped his beer, he thought about the liquor and everything else he'd given up. And maybe because he and Naomi had talked about her the other day, he had a clear vision of Elizabeth Madison, the woman he'd become involved with after Jayne left him, handing him a rocks glass full of booze….

She'd sat on her white leather couch, a martini, dry, two olives, in her hand. Funny, he remembered the pretty ice-blue dress she'd been wearing. "Here you go, darling. You seem like you could use reinforcements." Her dark looks always pleased him, as did her refinement. Her sophistication had reminded him of Jayne. At one time, he thought he wanted that in a woman.

"I'm thinking of leaving New York, Elizabeth."

She'd studied him carefully. "Look, I know you're upset about Tim. But forsaking everything you've built up here is foolish."

"Timmy's not the only reason I want out. I hate this life now."

"You'll get over that." She moved in close. "And I'm here."

"I thought you'd come with me." He had picked up her hand and rubbed the obscenely expensive diamond he'd given her. "We could settle in Riverdale. Raise our kids there. A big city like this is no place to have a family."

Drawing back, she'd peered down her nose at him. In bed she was hot and needy. Outside of the bedroom, she could turn as cool as a February night. "I was raised here."

It took him a while before he realized what she was saying, what ultimatum she was giving him. He called her on it, and she refused to leave with him. They'd parted with hard feelings, even though her father had understood Luke's need to go home.

"Hey, boss. Where are you?"

He looked up to find Ranaletti had joined him at the bar. "Nowhere important."

"Thinking about Her Highness?"

"Nope."

Ranaletti took a seat next to him. The guy was about his height, but thinner. "How long is she sticking around?"

"I'm not sure. I didn't bring her to the job."

"Jess did. I don't blame him. She looks like that old movie star…what was her name?"

"Elizabeth Taylor."

Some of his other men had moved in closer. One, Zeke Huff, a bulky son of a bitch who helped out on the electrical stuff with Cal, wasn't Luke's favorite person. He'd had run-ins with the guy on many Harmony Housing jobs. Zeke must have overheard Ranaletti's comment, because he said, "She's a nice piece, all right. Got Jess pussy-whipped."

"Watch what you say, Huff. Rumors hurt people."

"What, you think somebody in here's gonna go running back to wifey and tell her Jess is thinkin' with his johnson?"

"I said shut the hell up!"

The man's dark eyes narrowed. "It ain't just me who noticed. It's happening all over the site. Now, if *you're* thinkin' about getting in her pants, that's a different story. I wouldn't mind some myself when you're done."

Luke scraped back the stool and stood. He wanted to rip the guy's face off for his crude comments about Jayne. The only thing that stopped him was the door opening, and Mick O'Malley stumbling through it. Mick scowled at Luke, made his way down the bar and took a seat. A different kind of emotion filled Luke. Guilt had him pulling his punch and turning to leave.

Outside Harry's, he leaned against the wall and closed his eyes, trying to quell the mix of emotions swirling inside of him. Rage over the crude remarks about Jayne. Anger at himself for caring.

And, of course, guilt. Because every time he saw Mick O'Malley, Luke was forced to confront the fact that he was responsible for Timmy's death.

CHAPTER FIVE

FROM JAYNE'S VIEWPOINT on the side porch, the backyard of Eleanor's house sparkled. Dusk was setting in and tiny white lights twinkled from the trees, while pretty paper lanterns hung from garden trellises and dotted the slate walkways snaking through the flower beds. Of course, Luke's gazebo, the generous gift he'd given *Miss Ellie* for her seventy-fifth birthday, was the focus of attention, garnering comments that stroked the man's ego. Which, Jayne thought, had grown so big it needed a good deal of reinforcement.

Despite her anger at his reaction to her suggestions about the house plans, she couldn't seem to take her eyes off him. He was so handsome tonight in a gauzy white shirt rolled up at the sleeves and knife-pressed dark slacks. She recalled how she'd loved his clothes in New York, told him how, sometimes, she couldn't wait to get him out of them.

To escape the thought, she turned her attention to his date. The striking redhead with skeins of hair falling down her back, exposed by the halter-top sundress, was beautiful and sophisticated. Was *she* taking those clothes off Luke these days? The notion hurt more than it should have, given how long it had been since Jayne had done that.

Behind her, a voice said, "Luke's got terrific taste in women, doesn't he?"

Touching her short locks, Jayne said to Jess, "She's beautiful."

"You are, too."

In the past few days, Jayne had bought some jeans and shirts to wear to the work site. She'd also splurged on a couple of dresses. The pale peach Ralph Lauren she wore tonight was silky and strapless. On her feet were high-heeled sandals.

"I thought I'd be a bit daring with this outfit."

"Not your usual style."

It wasn't. Her taste ran to designer suits for work in several colors and styles, and black dresses when she had to go out at night. She wondered why she'd chosen something so different. Her gaze strayed to Luke again. Dear God, had it been for him?

"Isn't the gazebo great?" Jess commented. "Luke's the most generous man I know." He studied the structure. "I think the posts should have been white, though."

Jayne laughed out loud. "He and I had words over that."

"You thought so, too?"

"Hmm."

Sliding his arm around her shoulders, Jess tugged her close. His affection so natural, as it had been years ago. "We always were in synch, kiddo."

"Jess?"

Naomi had come to the French doors facing the side of the house. Turning, Jayne saw she was dressed in a short white skirt and camisole of steel-blue, which went beautifully with her eyes and Florida tan. Jayne told her so, and the woman's response was a crisp thank-you.

"Come out here, honey."

Naomi stepped onto the porch a discreet distance away. Leaving Jayne's side, Jess went to his wife and circled an arm around her shoulders. She remained stiff and scowling, making Jayne tense. Their proximity wasn't pleasant for either of them, Jayne suspected. She was just about to excuse herself when someone she didn't know came up to them.

"Jess, we need more beer in the cooler. Want me to get it?"

"No thanks, Joe. I'll take care of it. I'm bartender tonight." He kissed Naomi's cheek. "Be right back."

When he left, Naomi started to move away, too. Before she could leave, though, Jayne grasped her arm. She hated these kinds of confrontations but felt compelled to have this one. "Could you wait a minute? I haven't had a chance to talk to you since I got here two weeks ago."

Now, Naomi faced her. Her skin was flushed and the expression in her eyes was…fearful. "What do we have to say to each other, Jayne?"

"I'm sorry if my being in town upsets you. And I know you can't like me working at the Harmony Housing site."

Naomi's face drained of color. "You're working at the site?"

"Y-you didn't know?"

"No, Jess didn't tell me." Her eyes filled. "Why are you here, Jayne? Why are you doing this to my family?"

Her heart began to beat fast. "I…I'm having a difficult time—"

"Are you so selfish to put your welfare above Jess's?"

That hurt, so she didn't respond.

Naomi wasn't done. "You dig yourself into a professional hole and all of a sudden you've got to see Jess. You're needy, Jayne, and seeking comfort. We all know who'll be the one to give it, just like he did in college."

"You only think that because of the men in your family." Feeling cornered, Jayne spoke without censoring her words.

"Oh, my God, you know about that?"

"Yes, and it's colored your view of me and Jess."

"You bitch."

"That's *enough!*"

Naomi stiffened at the sound of Jess's voice. When Jayne looked over, she took a sharp breath. She'd never seen Jess so infuriated, not even when they were falsely accused of cutting corners in college.

He said, "I have never done anything to dishonor you, Naomi."

"You've got to be kidding me." Naomi's voice rose a notch. "You tell this woman all my private business, and then you *don't* tell *me* she's working at the site. Is that honoring me?"

"You can guess why I didn't say anything. You're behaving badly."

Naomi gasped.

Jess nodded to Jayne. "I apologize for my wife." He turned and went into the house.

"Don't you dare walk away from me, Jess Harper." Naomi started after him. "I haven't…" The rest trailed off when she disappeared through the French doors.

Defeated, Jayne leaned her head against the porch post. Well, that was it. There was no way she could stay in Riverdale now.

FROM INSIDE his gazebo, Luke watched the scene unfold on Miss Ellie's side porch and swore.

"Don't hold back, Luke."

Hell, he'd forgotten Elise was with him. Of course, he'd been tracking Jayne all night long. "I'm sorry. That was crude. I just can't believe how much trouble one woman can cause."

Elise lifted a bare shoulder. "Eleanor doesn't think so. Her face lights up every time she looks at…what's her name?"

"Plain Jayne."

With the confidence of a beautiful woman who wasn't afraid to recognize others' attractiveness, Elise laughed. "You need glasses if you think that."

Okay, so she was a knockout in the damn dress that bared her shoulders and upper chest. It made him drool and he imagined every other red-blooded man at the party was having the same reaction. Someone else approached her. Mick O'Malley. He gave her a big smile and held out his hand. Jayne shook it. Mick leaned in close, but Jayne's back was to the post and Luke couldn't see if she wanted to escape the pretty damn obvious invasion of her personal space. As he watched Mick, something came to him.

The guy had resented the hell out of Luke all through their childhood and had never missed a chance to needle him. He wouldn't choose Luke for his team in any kind of pickup game; he made up excuses why Luke couldn't talk to Timmy when he called the O'Malley house. And, routinely, he went after girls that Luke showed an interest in. What was Mick thinking now? Maybe nothing. Maybe he was just fawning over a beautiful woman with all that exposed skin.

The longer Luke watched them, the more it became

obvious that Mick was drunk. Again. Just like his father. Timmy had spent much of his time at the Corelli house because he and his brother lived in fear of Paddy O'Malley's fists. Had they ever invited Mick to be part of that respite?

"Who's the guy with her?" Elise asked.

"Mick O'Malley. The brother of one of my best friends." Elise was new in town, having come to Riverdale Glass as an engineer this year, so she didn't know all his relationships with people in town.

She touched his arm. "The one who died?"

Jayne pushed away from the post and turned so Luke could see her better. Her smile was stiff and forced, probably due to the tiff she'd had with Naomi.

"Luke? I asked about your friend."

"Yes, Timmy's the one who died."

And the man flirting with Jayne blamed him. On more than one occasion, Mick had attacked him. *You bastard. You're responsible for Timmy's death.*

To which Luke had no retort because, ultimately, he believed he *was* responsible.

"Luke, are you all right?"

"Yeah, I need another beer. Want something?"

"No thanks."

"I'll be right back."

Preoccupied, he made his way across the lawn where he met up with his sister Corky and her oldest son, Louie.

She kissed him on the cheek. Her eyes seemed sad and he could tell she was tired. "Your gazebo is beautiful."

"Thanks." He socked Louie's arm. The boy looked just like Cal, with sandy-brown hair and hazel eyes. "Hey there, kid."

"Hi, Uncle Luke." His tone was off.

"Something wrong?"

Louie shrugged. "Dad didn't come home after work. He was supposed to be here with us."

Corky's face reddened. "He was seeing an old friend."

That sounded strange. Before Luke could ask about it, his high school math teacher approached him. Small towns, he thought as his sister excused herself and Mr. Lawson asked him about building a new deck. When Luke finally arrived at the porch, Mick was at the bottom of the steps at the cooler.

Lifting the lid, he grumbled, "Where the hell is the beer?" Then he saw it was Luke next to him. His expletive was cruder than Luke's earlier slip had been.

Up close, Luke noted that Mick's eyes were glazed and he was slurring his words. The guy was drunker than Luke had realized. "Doesn't look like you need more. If you want a ride home, I'll take you."

Mick's hands fisted at his sides. "Why, so you can plow into a tree and kill off another O'Malley?" Shaking his head, he stumbled away.

Luke felt like pond scum.

But the birthday girl came up to him, forcing him to pretend he was all right. She frowned down at the cooler. "Luke, dear, could you get some…oh, what's wrong?"

He stared after Mick. "Nothing."

A gentle hand on his arm. "He's suffering, even after all these years. As you are."

Luke sighed. What could any of them say? Instead, he pointed at the cooler. "I'll get more beer."

Miss Ellie gave him a comforting squeeze. "I asked Jess to do it. I wonder why he didn't."

He was too busy fighting with Naomi. "I think he and Naomi went for a walk."

"How nice. They need time alone together."

Luke excused himself and took the stairs to the porch. Inside, as he opened the fridge, he heard scraping overhead. Someone was in the house, in the room above the kitchen. Closing the refrigerator, he walked into the living area and climbed the spiral oak staircase that not too long ago he'd helped Jess strip and restain. At the end of the corridor, in the room over the kitchen, a door was ajar and someone was rummaging around. He hurried to the entrance.

The desk was at an odd angle, as if she'd attempted to move it, but now Jayne was standing on the chair trying to get something from a high shelf in the closet. She was yanking on it when, suddenly, the chair swiveled.

"Oh," she said as she began to fall.

Leaping across the distance between them, Luke caught her before she hit the ground. Unfortunately, her foot snagged in the arm of the chair. Then the thing swiveled again, knocking both of them off balance and onto the floor. He managed to take the brunt of the fall and landed on his back with her on top of him. At the physical contact, the first between them in years, he was swamped by associations, by memories, by the pure joy of holding her again.

But her violet eyes were wide with fear and she was trembling. Instead of railing at him for trying to help her, this time she buried her face in the folds of his shirt. The gesture was so tender, so familiar, he found himself cupping her head with one hand and sliding his other arm around her. His fingers brushed the creamy skin bared by her dress. Her shoulders and her back were soft as silk.

Unfortunately, Luke felt himself go hard.

WHEN JAYNE'S HEART calmed down, she became aware of Luke. The feel of his muscular chest covered in soft material beneath her cheek. One arm banded around her. Her breasts pressed into him. Then there was his smell—oh, dear Lord—it was so sexy. And just like before, the combination of all that maleness made her go damp. She was helpless to draw away, until she became aware of *his* reaction below the belt. It took her a moment before she realized that their mutual response was *not* a good idea.

"Damn it," she said.

The rest of his body tensed. "Look, it's no big deal," he barked. "It's not like this hasn't happened before."

His dismissal of his reaction to her hurt, but she covered it with bravado. "We are so done with that. Control your hormones." She scrambled off him and stood. Or tried to stand, before she toppled onto him again.

And again, the part of him that was indeed very male reacted. He was shockingly aroused this time.

"What the hell's the matter with you?" he asked.

"I must have twisted my ankle. It's too weak to stand on."

With a curse, he eased her to the floor and rolled to his feet. Then he scooped her up.

"What are you doing?"

He set her on the bed. "Don't get your panties in a twist. I'm just—" His comment stopped abruptly and his gaze narrowed on her. "You, um, better fix that."

"Fix what?"

He nodded to her chest. She looked down. The bodice of her dress had slipped, revealing most of her breasts. "Oh." She yanked the material up into place and held her hand there.

Seeming nervous, Luke averted his gaze. He caught sight of the closet. "What the hell were you doing up there on a goddamned chair that swivels?"

"I tried to move the desk but could hardly budge it, and the chair was the only other thing in the room to stand on. I was trying to get my suitcase down. Jess put it up on one of those high shelves."

"Why'd you want your suitcase?"

She glanced at her phone on the night table. "Because I'm leaving Riverdale on a red-eye tonight."

His brow furrowed. "Just this week you said you were staying."

She shook her head. "I'm causing Jess too much trouble. No matter what you think of me, I love him like a brother and I won't bring more unhappiness on him than I already have. I saw clearly tonight that I shouldn't have come."

"Where will you go?"

"It doesn't matter."

"Of course it does." Jess's voice came from the doorway. "You're staying right here, Jaynie."

Both Jayne and Luke looked over at a clearly annoyed Jess. "You're not going MIA from my life again for six years."

"Yes, I am. I can't stand watching you and Naomi fight over me."

"We aren't going to be fighting over you anymore."

"Why?" Luke asked, his tone suspicious.

"Because I'm moving out of the house on Second Street for a while."

"What?" Luke said.

Jayne gasped. "Oh, Jess, you can't do that."

"I already have."

"Where are you gonna stay?" Now Luke's voice was filled with anger.

"Right here, in my old room."

"Down the hall from Jayne? Oh, yeah, Jess, this is a great idea. Just great."

"Don't say another word. You're risking our friendship. With Timmy gone, you can't afford to lose me, too."

Luke froze. Jess mirrored him, looking unbelievably chagrinned.

And Jayne asked, "What do you mean? What happened to Timmy?"

BEREFT, LUKE SAT in the gazebo at eleven that night. All of the guests had found their way out, even Elise, who'd gone home a half-hour ago, leaving him alone with his misery. Jess was right. He'd lost Timmy through his negligence, and now he was on the brink of losing Jess, too. Though he'd never expected an attack from the very man who'd tried tirelessly to convince Luke he'd been innocent in Timmy's death, he deserved it. In spades.

He heard a rustle and saw Jayne limping toward him with a suitcase in her hand. She reached the gazebo, stepped inside and set the case down. Moonbeams kissed her shoulders like a lover might. Damned if he could stop his reaction to her again. Still, he could be civil.

She said, "I, um, I'd like to talk to you."

"I know. I'm an ass. I made Jess choose and he chose you."

Dropping onto the bench next to him, she ran a hand through her hair, messing it. "I think this goes deeper for Jess. He hates it when he feels people he loves are being unfair to him. In college, when our friends turned on us, he couldn't deal with it. Because he's so loyal and trustworthy, he expects everyone else to be." She cleared her throat. "You and Naomi, especially."

Luke started to speak but she held up her hand.

"No, it doesn't matter anymore. I came out here to tell you I'm still leaving on that red-eye."

"Despite Jess's objections?"

"Yes." She indicated the suitcase. On top of it was her purse. "I know you don't believe me, but I never wanted to cause trouble. Like I said earlier, I love Jess too much to stay now."

He just watched her, his emotions playing paddleball with each other. He didn't want her to go, and he didn't want her to stay.

"I need to know something, though, before I leave."

"What?"

"What happened to Timmy? Did you have a falling-out?"

Again, Luke froze, just like up in the bedroom.

"I asked Jess about him but he wouldn't talk about it."

Still, Luke couldn't answer.

"I mentioned it but we were interrupted. Then I got so caught up in what was going on with me…" She halted. "Luke, what's wrong?"

Luke shook his head and felt his eyes mist. She must have caught on and touched his arm. "Luke, what happened?"

Suddenly, the words he'd said to no one, the whole sordid story that he hadn't told to a single soul, just tumbled out.

"We were so young, Jayne, for all that success, after we went to Dubai."

"Why did you go? I never knew."

"I wrecked my knee playing football. It healed enough to run and stuff, but no contact sports, so my college scholarship went down the tubes. Mom and Dad would have helped, but Dad had just had his first bypass surgery and I couldn't burden them with this. I told them I was hot to go overseas."

"You weren't?"

"In some ways I was. I loved my family and didn't really want to leave them. But I wanted fame and fortune, too."

"All kids do."

"Timmy especially." He told her about Paddy O'Malley's abuse.

"So you went to get him out of that situation?"

"Partly. It's another thing Mick holds against me. We left him here alone to protect his mother and himself." He shook his head in disgust. "Anyway, we made scads of money, banked it, and after four years, returned to the States."

"That's when you joined Madison Conglomerates?"

"Yes. They wanted to make us junior partners because we had the upfront money. So we made a ton more."

"You seemed to handle it okay."

"I did. But Timmy didn't. He loved the high life a little too much."

"He was a partyer when I knew him, but not to that degree."

"He got worse after you left." He swallowed hard. "God, this is hard. I think it started to go bad while you were still in New York. I just didn't notice." Unable to help himself, he reached out and ran a hand down her hair. "I got involved with you, spent all my time with you, and neglected him. I didn't see it happening, Jayne, I didn't."

"Oh, Luke. I'm so sorry."

"For a while after you left, I wasn't fit company for anybody. I threw myself into my work. Once I shaped up, and realized that Timmy was in way over his head, I tried to talk to him. He got surly, moody and mad at me. All I did was alienate him more, so he didn't tell me much. After a while, we only saw each other at work, and he functioned there, too. I thought, screw it, if he doesn't want to be friends, so be it. I'd live my own life."

"What happened to change that?"

"He got deeper into drugs and eventually needed more to feed his habit, so he came to me for help."

"That's good."

"No, not help in getting clean. He wanted money from me. He'd blown all his cash on drugs and gambling, which I didn't even know he was into."

"Oh."

"I said no to the money." God, he could still see Timmy's dark eyes, bloodshot and watery, his shoulders hunched, his tone pleading. "But I told him I'd do anything to help him get straight. He left my place saying he'd think about it."

"Did he get help?"

Luke's throat clogged. He couldn't answer.

Jayne drew back and faced him. "What? Tell me."

"He went back to his place, got his Rolex watch to sell and scored—for the last time."

"He overdosed? Timmy's *dead?*"

Feeling his eyes spill over, he nodded. "I was the last person to see him alive. I…if I hadn't…" Luke couldn't get it out. "I should have…"

Jayne grasped his shoulders. "Done what? What could you have done?"

"Stopped him."

"You tried."

"Maybe not hard enough."

"Luke, you know that one person can't make another get clean and sober."

"I do here," he said pointing to his head. "Not here." He laid his palm over his heart.

She put her hand over his. "You just need to let your heart catch up. I'm so, so sorry about Timmy. He was a great guy. But his downslide wasn't your fault."

"If I hadn't been so obsessed with you…"

"You were obsessed with me?"

"Yeah, of course."

"I never knew."

"It doesn't matter. I'm not blaming you, though seeing you again has reopened old wounds."

She sighed. "All the more reason for me to leave."

Luke was touched by her conciliatory tone and unselfish gesture. "I—"

Her phone shrilled into the darkness from her purse.

"Who'd be calling you this late?" he asked.

"I don't…oh, wait, it's only eight in California. It must be…" She drew in a heavy breath, got up, fished out the phone and tentatively said into it, "Jayne Logan."

Luke watched her face in the lamplight from the gardens. Her complexion had gone white. "Hello, Michael. I take it you have news."

As she listened, her only reaction was to grip the phone; then she turned away from Luke. "Yes, yes, I understand. No, I know it's not. Yes, of course. I'll be in touch." She clicked off, slipped the phone into the dark slacks she'd changed into and kept her back to him.

When Luke saw her shoulders begin to shake, he got up and crossed to her. Placing his hands on her upper arms, he was about to speak when she said, "Don't," and tried to draw away.

He held on tight. "Bad news?"

She nodded.

He could feel the emotion welling up and out of her, feel her body quiver with it. And he couldn't stand it. "How bad?"

Clearing her throat, she said, almost inaudibly, "Very bad."

He let it go a few seconds, and when she didn't say more, he tugged her around. "Tell me."

She wasn't crying, but her eyes were so bleak it killed him. "That was my lawyer. The architectural board called him. The Coulter Gallery…the walkway that collapsed…"

"What did they find?"

"It was my fault. There was an error in the design. Michael didn't know the technical details and they're sending me an official report. Oh, dear Lord, Luke, I made a mistake!"

Once again his former feelings for this woman surfaced. He had to help. "Look, Jayne, we all make mistakes."

"No, this is really bad. The next step is the board investigation into whether I'm guilty of gross negligence or understandable error. Or fraud, which it wasn't, on my part at least. Still, I could be blamed in a lawsuit." She took in a breath. "If any of the above happens, I'll have my architect's license revoked."

"I'm so sorry, honey."

She glanced at her suitcase and seemed to shutter her emotions right before his eyes. Throwing her head back, she straightened. "No matter, I'm still leaving. I reserved a ticket to Florida, and now I'm glad. I can't go back to California and face this." *Alone* would have been the next word in her sentence.

Images surfaced of those weeks after Timmy died, when Luke had come back to Riverdale.

His entire family had rallied around him. If it hadn't been for them, he wouldn't have made it through the ordeal.

First his father had tried to drag him out of his funk. *Luciano, I will not have this. People are responsible for their own actions. Have we not taught you this?*

Then his mother gave her advice. *My poor baby—being the only boy has made you too sensitive about protecting others.*

But it had been his four beautiful sisters who made the biggest difference—Corky spending nights with him so he wouldn't drink himself into oblivion; Teresa, a stay-at-home mom, cooking meals and insisting he eat. Even Maria took a long vacation from her corporate job to hold his hand through the grieving process. And of course Belle, who reamed him out and hugged him in the same breath. All of them had lifted him from the pit of despair.

"No way. You aren't leaving."

"What?"

"Stay here with people who'll help you deal with this thing."

Her brow furrowed. "I don't understand. You've wanted me gone since the day I got here. And now, after what you told me about Timmy, I'm obviously just bringing back your guilt. It's best for everybody if I go."

"When Timmy died, I wanted to die along with him. Seriously. Instead, I came home. My family and friends saved my life."

"That's a different thing. I don't belong in Riverdale."

"You have people who love you here—Jess and Miss Ellie. I'll help, too. I'll patch it up with Jess, and try to make Naomi see reason. Or maybe even talk them into counseling."

"You can't fix everything, Luke. You always thought you could, but it's an illusion."

Reaching out, he gave her hand a squeeze. "I know. Sorry, it's a bad habit. But you're staying."

God, he hoped he was doing the right thing. For the sake of Jess and Naomi, she really should leave town, yet he simply couldn't let her go. She was suffering and it cut him to the core.

But there was something else—something he'd been forced to admit when he saw her again, something that had been exacerbated when he held her in his arms earlier tonight. He wanted her back in town. Back in his life. That was so not good for him or for Jess, and probably not for her. Still, that was how he felt, and he couldn't do anything about it.

CHAPTER SIX

As JAYNE RAN through the streets of Riverdale, the May sunrise kissed the newly mowed lawns and budding treetops, making her glad she'd worn light fleece running shorts and a cool T-shirt. She was rounding the corner of Eighth Street onto Chestnut when she spied a jogger in the distance. No one else had been hitting the pavement at this hour—she'd left the house at six—but maybe it was late enough now for others to take a Saturday morning jog. So much had happened to bring her out here—the pronouncement of her guilt in the building walkway's collapse; the run-in with Naomi that caused Jess to leave his house; and, finally, Luke's horrific news that Timmy was dead.

She could still see him, tears in his eyes, his shoulders hunched, confessing what he thought was his role in Timmy's death. Until she'd gotten her own life-altering phone call. Then he'd tried to comfort *her* and ended up encouraging her to stay in town. She'd been dumbfounded.

The desire she'd been trying to keep at bay since she'd come to Riverdale and found him here, since she'd been confronted by his masculine presence, had been heightened by falling into his arms in the bedroom. Then, when he'd held her in the gazebo, she'd felt encompassed by him, supported, understood, empathized with. And, dangerously, protected, something she hadn't allowed herself to experience with any man since…Ben. Not even in New York, with Luke, had she let herself go as she had in college. But now, if she stayed in Riverdale, how she would deal with all the renewed feelings for Luke swirling inside her?

The jogger came closer, and she was shocked to see it was Jess. Her heart began to beat fast—she'd have to tell him about the mistake she'd made in the design of the Coulter Gallery, and she wasn't sure she had the strength to give him more bad news. Poor Jess had enough on his emotional plate.

"Hey, there, sweetie," he said when he reached her. "You went out early."

Halting in front of him, she tried to give him a smile. It felt as phony as the one on his face. "Hi, Jess. Yeah, I didn't sleep well."

"You didn't sleep at all." At her frown, he added, "I didn't, either."

"I'm sorry. I know it must be hard to be away from Naomi. You should go back home."

"*You* should have come down the hall and told me about the findings of the architectural board."

Her brows shot up. "You know?"

"Uh-huh. I went out to the gazebo and sat with Luke most of the night."

Soon after hearing the news from her lawyer, Jayne had gone to bed and assumed Luke had left Eleanor's. "So he told you?"

Jess nodded. "I think he wanted to spare you having to tell it all again." He squeezed her arm. "Come on, let's walk. You're done running for now." They started down the road.

"Luke encouraged me to stay in Riverdale, Jess."

"I know. He's hotheaded and he can be rash about things, but he's a fair guy most of the time."

"Most?"

"I've never been crazy about how he handles the women in his life. He says he's changed since Timmy's death, but who knows."

Now, she guessed, wasn't the time to tell Jess she'd been one of those women.

"He's always been a love-'em-and-leave-'em kind of guy, and hasn't ever really gotten involved with anyone."

Jess had told her that years before she ever met Luke. It was one of the reasons she'd tried to stay detached in New York, and maybe one of the reasons she'd run from Luke. Hadn't she wondered what he saw in her, and if he'd leave her like Ben had?

"Do you think he was sincere about my staying?"

"I hope so. I can't imagine why else he'd say what he did." Jess frowned. "He's made mistakes, too, and he knows what it's like to need the comfort of family around."

"I'm not family."

Jess gave her a brief hug. "Of course you are."

"Jess, he told me about Timmy."

Jess stopped short and his face flooded with emotion. "Are you kidding? He never talks about Timmy to anybody, not even me."

"I knew Timmy in New York, when I worked with them on Madison Conglomerates projects. I had no idea he was in such bad shape."

If possible, Jess looked even sadder. "Nobody did. Not even Luke. He blames himself, but he gets pissed off when I bring it up." He ran a hand through his hair.

"I guess I don't like to talk about it, either. I should have told you about Timmy when you asked that day in the trailer, but this is hard for me to talk about, too."

"I should have pursued it, but things got crazy. I feel so self-absorbed."

"I—"

"No, you don't have to make me feel better about this, Jess. We don't have to talk about it now, either, not when your life is upside down. Just know how sorry I am."

"Man, everything's such a mess."

"What are you going to do about Naomi?"

"I decided last night that all I've done is mask this problem for years. I gave it a shot her way, but she reneged on our agreement. End of story. We'll have to work out her lack of trust whether or not you're in town, Jaynie." He shrugged, but Jayne could hear the sorrow in his voice. "I'm going over today to see if I can explain why I feel she's being unfair. Maybe clearing the air will help."

"Oh, good." They reached the house. Again, just the sight of it made Jayne feel better. Being near her favorite buildings had that effect on her. The thought only underscored the precariousness of her situation.

"What's next from the architectural board?" Jess asked.

"My lawyer received the preliminary findings. He'll get the official report sometime next week with the specifics of what went wrong. I also hired an independent firm to do an analysis, and I'm assuming they'll come to the same conclusions. Then the board has to decide if I'm guilty of fraud, negligence or simply an error in judgment."

"We know it wasn't fraud."

"But if it's gross negligence, I'm sunk."

"You're anything but grossly negligent. It was a mistake."

"Even if it was just that, Jess, my reputation is tainted, maybe beyond repair."

Jess didn't say anything. One thing she valued about him was that he never offered false hope or platitudes. When they'd been betrayed in college, he hadn't made excuses for Ben and Sally.

Finally, he said, "I guess you'll have to find a way to deal with that next." He grasped her hand. "I've been giving this some thought, Jayne. Were there any changes made to your original blueprints?"

"Yes, of course, there are always changes. Builders find easier ways to put up walls for rooms, engineers discover how the internal structure *should* be changed. And the electrician needs to reroute some wiring. I've never worked on a building that didn't have any last-minute alterations."

"And you signed off on them for the Coulter Gallery?"

"I have to. What are you getting at?"

"I wonder if the error occurred there. Maybe it was a decision that could have gone either way, so you made changes that weren't, in the long run, right."

"I looked at the final alterations and didn't see anything."

"Maybe you need a fresh pair of eyes. Do you have the plans with you?"

"I do, back at the house."

"Including what was changed?"

"Yes, I'm meticulous about record keeping."

"Let's go take a look at them, in light of what we talked about."

Again, she felt better. Jess could always do this for her. And, by God, she needed him now.

By eight o'clock, they were at the kitchen table,

drinking coffee and poring over the changes she'd made in the blueprints. Jess was frowning at them.

"Do you see something?" she asked nervously.

"Maybe. Look at these three."

Jayne scanned the changes he'd highlighted. "I considered these already and dismissed them."

"Why?"

"Because I suggested two of them and knew those were better than the original. The change in the rods was the structural engineer's idea. He had research on why his change was viable and, though I didn't like him much, he was very good at his job."

"Okay. Let's look further."

A half hour later, Eleanor shuffled in wearing a light robe and slippers. "Good morning." She spied the plans. "That's a lot to be tackling at this hour."

"We were, um, up early," Jayne said self-consciously.

Crossing to the sink, Eleanor put water in the teakettle and transferred it to the stove. Then she came to stand by the table. "Did something happen I don't know about?"

"I'm afraid so. I got the results of the architectural board's inquiry last night." In halting sentences, Jayne explained the situation. "We're going over the plans now to see if the error might have been related to some changes that were made to the original plan."

The older woman squeezed her shoulder. "I'm so sorry, dear. I know how much this must hurt."

A lump the size of a golf ball formed in her throat. The reality that she *had* made a mistake was almost untenable this morning.

The teakettle whistled. Eleanor fixed herself a cup, then returned to the table and sat. "We'll all help you through this, Jayne." She zeroed in on her son. "Now, let's talk about you, Jess."

Jess tried to smile, but his shoulders slumped with the weight of all that had happened. In the bright light coming from the windows, his face was etched with lines of fatigue. "I'm fine, Mom."

"I need to say something." Eleanor sipped her tea, then blotted her mouth with a napkin. "Last night, you told me Naomi took the car and went home because she was tired. You stayed because you weren't ready to leave the party."

They'd made up that excuse so as not to ruin Eleanor's celebration.

"Yeah?"

"I don't like being lied to."

"Lied to? I—"

Eleanor held up her hand. "Don't compound what you've already done, young man. You and Naomi have both been lying to me for years."

Jayne dropped the pen she'd been writing with onto the yellow legal pad in front of her.

"I'm old, not senile."

Like two chastised children, Jess and Jayne exchanged a guilty look and kept quiet.

"I know about Naomi's objections to your relationship with Jayne, Jessie. I know you, Jayne, stopped coming to Riverdale because of Naomi's feelings. I've known all along you didn't abandon me."

"Why haven't you said anything before this?" Jess asked.

"Because it wasn't my place. I felt that you and Naomi needed to work things out in private. If you didn't tell me about the trouble, you didn't want me to know. And I realize Naomi was afraid your conflict would affect our relationship. Now, things have changed." Again, she took a bead on her son. "You didn't stay over here for one night, did you?"

"No, I've left the house for a while."

"I'm very sorry to hear that."

"Mom, I—"

"No, honey, I'm not criticizing. You have to do what you think is best. I just hate that it's gone this far. But it is what it is." Her favorite phrase. "And I trust you'll do the right thing."

"I'll have to tell Naomi that you know about what really happened."

"I realize that. And I'm sorry. This kind of situation is hard for her because of her father and her brother. I understand her point of view, but for what it's worth, I'm not happy that she's lumped *you,* a man of integrity like your dad, with them."

"Oh, Mom, don't turn on her. She'll need you, too."

"I'm doing no such thing. But I have to say what I feel. I'm not going to turn on her, you—" she looked at Jayne "—or you, Jaynie."

"Thank you, Eleanor." She bit her lip. "I can't tell you how much that means to me." Almost as much as Luke's support had.

At the thought of him, Jayne felt uneasy again. She'd have to keep his actions last night in perspective. She had no intention of depending on him, depending on any man for emotional support. If she decided to stay, she'd have to be very careful around Luke.

AT THE CRACK of dawn on Monday morning, Luke pulled up to the Harmony Housing site, got out of his truck and, carrying a much-needed hot black coffee, slammed the door. The sound echoed in the silence of the deserted lot. He'd had a shitty weekend, waiting for Jess to call him. Jess hadn't, and Luke had been preoccupied through the traditional Sunday dinner at his parents' house. Hell, at the browbeating of his sisters, he'd even agreed to chauffeur his nieces and nephews to the baseball game this Saturday. That should be fun, though.

Taking pleasure in the sweet scent of sawdust, more noticeable when men and machinery weren't on site, he walked around the perimeter of the house, thinking about what he'd done Friday night—telling Jayne about Timmy, breaking down, for God's sake, and then encouraging her to stay.

When he'd held her close after that damned news she'd gotten, he'd been swamped by old associations, enough to awaken in the wee hours of the morning from an incredibly erotic dream about Jayne—he'd taken off that mouthwatering dress in Miss Ellie's gardens while the sun gleamed off her like she was some classical statue. When he'd touched his fill, she was all his again.

Sinking onto a stack of lumber, he sipped from his cup. Okay, so he still wanted her. Why not? Wouldn't any man? Hadn't his crew, in their crude way, proved that? So Luke's response to her was just normal. He could control it. He had to. He couldn't let this attraction go anywhere, for a lot of reasons.

First off, it would only complicate the issue if Luke confessed his previous relationship with Jayne to Jess. Who knew how his friend would react? Or how Naomi would? But it was more than that. Because of Jayne's background, because she'd grown up in an emotionally sterile environment, she'd always kept her emotions controlled. Until she'd met that fool Ben. After his desertion, she became even more closed off. Luke had been making headway in New York—he was the exact opposite because of his upbringing—and she'd been starting to open up. But in the end, Jayne had left him because of the problem with Prentice Architects. And she'd hurt him deeply; it had taken him a long time to get over it.

He shook his head as he stared into the foundation. Jayne Logan was a runner—she'd run from him in New York, and hadn't she just escaped California when another issue had come up? Nope, he had to keep his distance, because chances were she'd run again if things got rough. And he didn't want to deal with the emotional fallout.

Feeling better, he reached into his pocket and took out today's to-do list. Hmm, they'd have to decide about the changes she'd suggested. He hadn't really given her plans serious consideration a few days ago. Maybe he'd better take another look.

Walking over to the trailer, he unlocked it and stepped inside. As coffee perked in the corner, he spread out the plans for the kitchen, put her notes next to them, and did a few preliminary sketches to see whether what she had in mind would work. He was vaguely aware of the trucks and cars arriving outside, the voices of his men, and the rumble of more lumber and equipment being unloaded.

After a while, he heard from the doorway, "Oh, hi."

He glanced up and his body jolted. She was wearing faded jeans that made her legs look a mile long. Her shirt was white and sported a picture of the Golden Gate Bridge. Under it was the slogan I "heart" My Architect. The soft-looking cotton accented her breasts.

Oh, yeah, sure, he was in control!

Struggling to stave off his physical reaction, he uttered, "Hi." The word came off gruffly, so he dialed down his tone. "You okay?"

"Yes. I got some sleep yesterday, and a good night's worth. Things always look better when you're rested."

"I know. When Timmy died, I became an insomniac. It wasn't until I started sleeping that I could see things more clearly."

She gave him a half smile. "Did your sisters engineer that, too?"

He couldn't help matching her smile. "Yeah, they wore me out with chores at their houses and babysitting their kids. They even forced me into some racquetball."

"Your sisters play?"

"Belle does. She beat the pants off me during that time."

"I saw her and the other three at Eleanor's party. They're all beautiful."

He stiffened.

"What's wrong?"

"Belle and Naomi are best friends."

"Ah. I guess I don't want to meet her, then."

Jayne was right about that. He hadn't told Belle about encouraging Jayne to stay in town. It hadn't been the time or place at his parents' Sunday dinner. Besides, he hadn't exactly worked out what explanation he could give without sounding like a traitor.

"So," he said in an effort to change the subject, "I've been looking at the suggestions you made for the interior layout of the houses."

Her face lit up, and Luke was hit with a blast of pure desire.

"Really? You were upset about my interference."

"Don't get me wrong, I don't like meddling. But I also want what's best for the people who will live here. Before we can go further, we have to decide if we're going to make any of the changes. I came in early and took a look."

She nodded to the legal pad. "What do you think?"

"Come over here. I'll show you."

She crossed the room and stood behind him. Damn, he thought she'd sit down. He could feel her whole body close to his, feel her breathing in, smell something on her—not perfume, perhaps shampoo or soap. It was feminine.

"Luke?"

He cleared his throat. "See this wall here you want moved?"

"Uh-huh."

"Snow in the winter will stress the joists too much if we change it."

"Ah, I should have thought of that. I'm not used to designing for this climate."

"But we can section off this part by adding a wall…" He pointed to the kitchen. "And then make a laundry/mudroom."

"That would work just as well."

Finally she took a seat beside him, which was a hell of a lot better. They spent the next hour discussing the changes to the rest of the house before Jess came in.

"Hi, guys."

Both looked to the doorway. Jess stood there, haggard and hunched, and anything but rested.

"Hey, buddy." Luke checked his watch. "You're late. Not like you."

"I took my girls to school."

"How'd it go?"

"They're confused. And scared." He stuck his hands in his pockets. "I hate that they're afraid because of something I did."

"Fear's a terrible emotion." This from Jayne.

"Let's not talk about it." He approached them. "What are you doing?"

When they told him, he dove right in. By nine, they had compromises worked out. Jayne objected to some of Luke's nay-saying, but he won and she agreed to do the schematics after she consulted with plumbers, electricians and a few others on the changes.

"What should I do today, Jess?"

"I got the volunteer list on my way in." He drew a paper out of his pocket and scanned it. "Mick O'Malley needs somebody to measure lumber for the downstairs. Want to do that until I find the contact information for the people you need to talk to?"

"I don't think she should—" Luke began.

But Jayne interrupted. "I can handle that." Standing, too, she reached for a hard hat from a stack on a nearby shelf. "Thanks, Luke, for listening to my opinions. See you guys later."

Luke watched her leave.

Jess said, "Thanks for being nice to her, buddy."

Luke grabbed his own hat and said, "No big deal." But before he left, he faced his friend. "Anything I can do? About Naomi?"

"Nah. It's all up to us." He nodded to the doorway. "Making Jayne's life easier would help me not worry so much about her, though."

"I think I can do that."

All morning Luke tried to ignore her. And all morning

he scanned the area to see where she was. He kept watching Mick O'Malley with her. And his temper began to seethe with each little observation—laughter coming from their direction several times, especially when Mick was the one to elicit it; Mick staring at her chest when she dropped the tape measure and bent over to pick it up. But when lunchtime came and Mick slid his arm around her and said something, making her smile, Luke had had enough. Angry, he stormed toward them. Even as he did, he wasn't sure exactly what he'd do or say.

"Um, no thanks," Jayne was saying. "I have some errands to run."

"You sure?" Mick asked smoothly. "I got enough lunch to share."

"You're sweet to offer, but no."

Both stopped talking—flirting—when Luke reached them. "How'd it go?" he asked.

Mick snorted. "As if you didn't know. I'll see you after lunch, Jayne." He squeezed her arm and left.

"What did he mean by that?" Jayne asked Luke.

"I have no idea." Which was a bald-faced lie. Mick had caught Luke staring at them. It burned him up to be so transparent, and so he snapped at her. "But a word of warning. Maybe it isn't a good idea to be so friendly with the guys on the site."

"What do you mean?"

"They're not used to working with women."

He could see her tense. "You're kidding, right? There are several female volunteers, and you've brought in a lot of women carpenters and construction workers in the last week. I...admired that about you."

"Yeah, but you're different."

She shook her head. "Damn it, Luke, I thought we were past this."

We were, until I saw you with Mick.

"You have to be one of the moodiest, most mercurial men I've ever met." When he didn't respond, she scowled fiercely, said, "I'm going to lunch," and stalked away.

As he watched her go, Luke cursed himself. Goddamn it, when *had* he become so clumsy and tongue-tied?

When Jayne had come back, that's when. Hell, he was jealous of Jess moving into the same house with her, and he'd been livid when Mick had fallen all over her this morning.

This was a fine mess.

FUMING, Jayne left Luke with long, angry strides. That man was infuriating! Why the hell would he be so nice to her on Friday night and this morning, then turn on her so quickly? He'd never been like this in New York. He wasn't like this around anyone else. If she hadn't been convinced before that she had to control this stupid attraction to him, she was now. She'd just reached the parking lot when a black Mercedes sports car pulled up beside her Lexus. Its sleek lines and inherent class matched its owner, who slid out of the front seat with the grace of a gazelle.

Jayne recognized Luke's girlfriend right away. She was dressed in a lovely brown and black print dress that was both sophisticated and sensual, with high black heels. Diamonds sparkled at her ears. Her red hair was drawn back in a clip that emphasized her high cheek-bones. "Hello. I'm Elise Jenkins."

Suddenly self-conscious of her jeans and T-shirt, Jayne gave her a weak smile. "Hi. I'm Jayne Logan."

"Yes, I know. Luke was talking about you at the party Friday night."

That was something to think about.

Elise's pretty auburn eyebrows furrowed. "He's been in a mood since then," she said as she bent over, slid up the front seat and drew a picnic basket out of the back seat. "So I brought him lunch."

"Sorry, but he's still in a foul mood."

"Oh, dear. Well, maybe I can—" she smiled slyly "—cheer him up."

Though her heart hurt at how Elise might make Luke feel better, Jayne managed to say, "Good luck with that."

"Thanks. Nice to meet you, by the way."

Elise's genuine warmth made Jayne feel bad for her negative thoughts. Hell, the woman was nice as well as glamorous.

"What's going on here?"

They both turned to see Luke a few feet away from them. His black T-shirt was damp and his hair mussed; he looked so good that a bolt of lust hit Jayne square in the stomach. All that masculinity approached Elise, and he enveloped her in a hug so warm and sexy it made Jayne's already bruised heart clutch in her chest.

Over Elise's shoulder, Luke stared right at Jayne. The creep. When he drew back, he bestowed an approving smile on the other woman. "Nice to see you, gorgeous."

"Really? Jayne said you were still in a bad mood."

"Jayne's wrong, I guess. Now that you're here, anyway."

Jayne wanted to cry. She wanted to throw something. She wanted to run from this scene. She decided on the latter. "I'll leave you two lovebirds alone." She gave as gracious a smile as she could to Elise. "Nice to meet you. Stick around if you can. Luke's almost human when you're here."

With that, she got in her car, started the engine and backed out. In the rearview mirror, she saw Elise slide her arm around Luke's trim waist and lean into him.

Jayne also saw Luke staring after *her* retreating car.

LUKE CHECKED the rearview mirror so he could see into the back of his dad's SUV. Behind him sat Teresa's three boys in the last row, ages ten, eleven and twelve. In front of them was one of Corky's girls with Maria's daughter, Analise. Belle's kids, Kasey, Karl and Kenny, were catching a ride to the ball field in Jess's van, along with Jess's girls. Luke had asked his best friend to help him drive the little ones. Man, he got a kick out of playing uncle.

"Ready, troops?"

"Yes, Uncle Luke," they chanted in unison.

"Rules of the road? Mikey," he called out to Teresa's oldest, "you give them."

"No yelling, slapping or mean words."

"Gotta be careful driving," Analise said. Truth be told, the towheaded eight-year-old was his favorite, because she was the spunkiest. He had a way with her, though.

With such precious cargo, Luke took it easy on the trip to the stadium where the Riverdale Royals, a farm team for a professional baseball outfit, would hold their first game of the season. Everybody loved baseball in his family and had passed the tradition down through the generations. He was doing his part today.

He was also doing penance. As he drove along side

streets, he thought of his confrontation with Belle, when she found out what he'd done…

Her face had flushed with anger. "What the hell are you doing, Luciano, telling that woman to stay in town?"

He'd asked himself the same thing a million times this week, when he'd tried to stay away from Jayne but hadn't managed to stop thinking about her. Still, he went to her defense with his sister. "She's at the lowest point in her life, Belle. She's about to lose the only thing she has left."

"Naomi's about to lose Jess."

"I don't think so. She and Jess will work this out."

"You don't know that. Damn, I can't believe…" Then that all-knowing gaze zeroed in on him. When they'd been young, Belle had been the sister who always sensed when he was up to something. "Don't tell me you…oh, God, Luke, you aren't interested in her, are you?"

"No!" But he reddened, and doing so belied his words.

"Hell! This is all we need to muck things up."

He agreed with Belle on that. He'd made a fool of himself at work this week, especially with his disastrous playacting with Elise. He couldn't believe he'd done that for Jayne's benefit.

"Damn it!" he said aloud.

"Ooo, Uncle Luke," Analise said. "No bad words."

"Right, sweetie. Sorry."

The little girl smiled at him in the rearview mirror. He knew she'd been corrected for her repetition of things she wasn't supposed to say.

When they arrived at the stadium, herding the kids

out of the van distracted him. Once in the stands, they paraded to their seats. When they neared their row, the first thing Luke noticed was Jayne, sitting next to Jess, with little Kasey on her lap. What the hell? Was someone trying to torture him by throwing her in his way?

The cousins greeted one another with cheers and high fives. "Okay, troops, sit." They filed in immediately. Despite the sour note of Jayne's presence, he had to smile. He loved how his nieces and nephews obeyed him.

Kissing Miss Ellie's cheek, he said curtly to Jayne, "I'm surprised to see you here."

To which she replied, "I was invited." She nuzzled Kasey's head. "Besides, I had to see the legendary Pied Piper in action."

There was a bit of jockeying for positions, but Luke managed to settle them all and make sure his own seat was down from and behind Jayne. When the game started, he kept one eye on the field and one on the kids. He did not look at Jayne's cargo shorts and the long legs they bared, or her white top with the lace neck, or the chain she wore—and where it nestled.

The game was good. The home team was running away with the score. Then Analise said, "I'm bored."

Luke suggested, "Come sit with me, then. We'll play I Spy."

The little girl climbed over her cousins, but instead of going to him in the next row up, she stood out on the steps and watched him. She made quite a picture in her denim jumper and bright pink sneakers, which matched her shirt. Defiance emanated from her very stance.

"Analise," he said softly.

"I don't wanna sit. I'm staying out here."

He stared at her.

Blue eyes stared back at him.

He cocked his head.

She raised her chin.

Then he gave her a half smile.

Finally, one appeared on her face. She threw herself onto his lap and he hugged her tightly.

After Analise sat, he glimpsed Jayne. Apparently she'd been watching the whole thing. *She* smiled—a big, beautiful smile filled with soft approval.

Damn it if he didn't bask in her reaction.

CHAPTER SEVEN

A FEW DAYS LATER, Jayne was unloading bags of plaster at the site when she saw Luke's truck pull into the lot. He was late this morning—very late—which was unlike him. As he climbed out of the front seat, she noticed right away what he was wearing. The most threadbare jeans she'd ever seen gloved his legs, and a ratty T-shirt with torn-off sleeves covered his torso. Even his hair was mussed. It hit her that he'd probably just rolled out of bed.

Whose? she wondered. The almost certainty that it was Elise's made her ill.

He crossed to her. "'Morning."

"Rough night?" she couldn't help asking him, but she hated the quiver in her voice.

"Not like you mean."

She cocked her head.

"Kenny, my sister's oldest, got in some trouble. He was caught drinking in the park with some other boys. I bunked at their place so Belle and Nick could go to the police station and deal with this."

Reaching out, Jayne squeezed his arm briefly. "Oh, Luke, I'm sorry. Is everything all right?"

"Yeah, he got off with a warning. But he's in hot water from drinking and being with kids he wasn't supposed to hang out with. Belle's furious."

Luke glanced down at his outfit with disgust. "Nick's clothes are too small for me and this is all I had left at her house." He ran a hand over his jaw. "No time to shave, either."

Which made him look dangerous. And sexy. What *was* it about that scruffy look on men?

"Everything okay here?"

"Uh-huh."

He eyed the bags. "That too heavy for you?"

Instead of getting angry, she was amused. "You just can't help yourself, can you?"

Before he could answer, another truck pulled up, this one battered and rusted; out of it slid Mick O'Malley, carrying two tall disposable cups. When he saw Luke, his gaze hardened. Ignoring Luke, he said, "Good morning, beautiful," to Jayne and handed her a cup. "Thought you'd like this."

"Why, thank you."

"I saw what you drank before." He gave her a small smile and walked away without acknowledging Luke's presence.

Jayne watched Luke as he stared after his best friend's brother, who hated him. Instead of peevishness, which she'd seen in him all week, his face was incredibly sad. "It must be hard dealing with his animosity every day."

"Nothing I don't deserve."

"You don't, Luke." When he didn't answer, she added, "Hey, what did you tell me the other night about making mistakes?"

He shrugged.

She arched an eyebrow. "It only works one way, huh, hotshot?"

His grin, framed by the growth of beard, was a killer. Jayne's whole body responded.

Trying to ignore her reaction, she held out the cup Mick had just given her. "I think you need this more than I do."

"Oh, man, do I. Thanks."

"You're welcome."

"I'd better go see what's happening here."

When he met with his crew, she could hear the teasing he endured about his lateness and his disheveled appearance. She noted he did nothing to refute the guys' innuendos about the way he'd probably spent his night.

Boys, she thought, and went back to her work.

After finishing her task, she was heading for the trailer when she caught sight of Luke bending over to pick up something on the ground. Three female workers around him turned to take in the view. Jayne was shaking her head at the leering—though she didn't blame them—when Luke's pants split right down the middle seam of his butt!

"Son of a bitch!" he spat out as he stood up quickly.

Whistles and catcalls erupted from the women.

Jayne herself began to giggle at what the split revealed: white jockey shorts, tight ones, with big red hearts on them. Probably undies his sisters had bought him, but Jayne wasn't going to tell anybody that. Instead, she joined, heartily, in the laughter aimed at his cute rear.

"WHAT THE HELL *is* this?" Luke yelled as he bolted up from the ground, where he'd just sat down in a pile of red ants. "The seven plagues of Egypt?"

From the blanket spread out by the tree, Miss Ellie

shook her head. "Luke dear, dust those off quickly. They bite."

"We told you to sit on the blanket," Jess offered. He seemed to be in a good mood today, more at ease with himself.

"There wasn't enough room." Not if he wanted to stay away from Jayne, at least, who leaned against the tree. She looked cool and comfortable; she'd taken off the overshirt she wore on the site, revealing a skimpy red tank top. Jess sat near her, and that unwanted flare of jealousy sparked again.

Today, right before lunch break, Miss Ellie had brought over a picnic for Jess and Jayne, and invited Luke to join in; he couldn't very well refuse. But he'd been trying to keep his distance from Jayne because, each day, he found it more difficult to resist her.

She'd given him Mick's coffee.

She'd been concerned about Kenny.

The look on her face when he'd ripped his pants two days ago had been more than amused. It had been... purely female.

And yesterday, when he'd walked under a ladder and stepped into a puddle from the rain the night before, splashing muddy water onto his clothes and even into his mouth, she'd gotten him a towel and pointed to the heavens. "Boy, who did you piss off up there?"

He was beginning to wonder about that himself. Especially after the ant attack, which Jess was still razzing him about. "You been a bad boy lately, Luciano?"

"No time. Between Belle's son and my dad's doctor's appointments, I've been busy."

"What's wrong with your father?" Miss Ellie asked solicitously.

"He had some angina a while back. Because of his bypass surgeries, I wanted to drive him myself to the doctor and the stress test."

"I hope he's okay," Jayne put in.

Luke did too. He was lucky to have his parents still living and couldn't even think about anything happening to them. It was bad enough worrying about his sisters' kids. Man, what would he do when he had his own?

As he dropped down on the edge of the blanket, he wondered if Jayne wanted kids. When he had brought it up once in New York, she avoided answering. But she'd been great with Kasey at the movies and the ball game. The little guy wouldn't go to anyone else so she held him the whole time, cooing and petting him.

An image of her with a belly swollen by a baby shocked Luke with its clarity. Son of a bitch! His imagination was way out of control.

"Hey, buddy," Jess said when he caught Luke staring into space. "You got a premonition of more things happening to you?"

Luke hoped to hell not.

ON SUNDAY MORNING when Eleanor and Jess were at church, Jayne headed outside to the gardens to water the plants. The rain earlier in the week hadn't been enough, and the trilliums needed a good soak. Because it was already hot outside, she'd thrown on a well-worn Cornell T-shirt with cutoff shorts. On her head she'd plopped an old baseball cap she'd dragged from the closet when she saw that the birds near the feeder had been *decorating* the yard.

Halfway through her task, a voice startled her from her thoughts. "Hey, there."

She turned around and found Luke. "You scared me."

He plopped his hands on hips covered with khaki shorts. A white T-shirt outlined his impressive chest. She studied him as he studied her. The May air got a lot warmer, and when their gazes met, his was sizzling. She adjusted the brim of her hat to break the spell.

"It's mine, you know," he said.

"What is?"

"The cap."

"Oh. You want it back?"

His expression was searing. "That's not what I want from you."

Ignoring the innuendo, she asked, "What are you doing up this early?"

"I came to fix a couple of shingles that are loose on the gazebo."

"Watch out." She nodded to the feeder, a big cedar thing that resembled a Buddhist temple. "The birds are all over the place today, which is why I put on your hat."

"You think you're talkin' to a sissy?"

"Suit yourself. With your luck this week, you might want to be careful." She couldn't help adding, "The girls at the site are still talking about your cute undies."

At the mention of underwear, Luke's gaze dropped to her breasts, making her conscious of the skimpy bra she'd put on today.

Turning away abruptly, he crossed to the shed, went inside and came out with a ladder. She gave him her back, but could picture him climbing the steps and eventually heard him hammering.

Lulled by the comforting sounds of building, she finished watering. She was heading to the faucet when she heard, "Shit, shit, shit!" She retraced her steps.

As she got closer to the gazebo, she could see her prediction had come true, and how appropriate Luke's curse had been. A pigeon had flown overhead and dropped his business right into Luke's thick, dark hair. He had no choice but to come down the steps.

She looked at the flowing hose in her hand. Well, hell, nobody could resist this. Creeping up to the ladder, she reached him just as he hit the ground. She lifted the hose and doused his head with cold water.

He bellowed…and pivoted fast.

All innocence, she said, "Just trying to help. The bird doo-doo's gone now, so—" The expression in his eyes made her stop mid-sentence.

Lightning fast, he wrested the hose from her and got off a shot that drenched her before she could get away. Still, she sprinted to the shed, darted in, shut the door and pulled a small wooden bench in front of it.

It was child's play for him to get inside.

Laughing, she backed up until she hit a worktable against the far wall. Luke just stood in the doorway, hose in hand, staring at her. From the light coming through the window off to the left, she could see his gaze level on her chest. She glanced down. Her breasts were outlined by the wet shirt, the lace of her bra visible; her nipples puckered.

When she looked back up at Luke, she heard him swear softly, toss the hose outside and, without breaking eye contact, close the door.

Then he advanced on her.

ACTING ON primal male instinct, Luke covered the distance to Jayne quickly. His heart was pumping and blood rushed in his head. When he reached her, he stood a few inches away, male to female, man to woman. Electricity sparked in the air. The dim light of the shed couldn't disguise her beckoning body and the desire emanating from her.

He lifted his hand and outlined the scoop of the T-shirt's neckline. The gasp that escaped her brought him potent satisfaction. "This is indecent," he said, his voice gravelly.

"Your fault."

A smile claimed his lips as his hand slid lower to her sternum. His splayed fingers spanned her chest. "I know, babe." He closed his hand over one breast. "You still want me."

Her eyes drifted shut and she sighed as he kneaded her. Though he wanted to rip off her shirt, he forced himself to go slow.

After a moment, she opened her eyes and circled his wrist with her fingers. Her face was flushed with arousal. Nonetheless, she whispered, "This is *so* not a good idea, Luke."

"Seems damned right to me." But since she'd protested, he found the will to ask, "Want me to stop?"

She moaned, fervently. "No."

He settled his other hand on her neck, anchoring her, and bent his head to kiss the bare skin exposed by her shirt.

At the once-familiar touch of his lips on her, he groaned. She tasted salty and earthy and, underneath that, the scent of her bath soap lingered. As if he had all day, and as if his body wasn't raging with need, his mouth traveled the expanse of skin to her right side. Then he buried his face in the crook between her shoulder and neck. She'd always liked that. He kissed her there. Bit lightly, making her jump. She grasped his shoulders as he soothed the nip with his tongue.

"Luke, please." He needed no more encouragement.

His hand slid from her neck to her head, and he gently drew it back by her hair, exposing her whole throat. He took his time there until she moaned again.

"What do you want, Jayne?"

"More" was all she muttered.

Moving in even closer, he plastered his body to hers, briefly basking in the curves and indentations, the soft suppleness of her. Bracing his arms on either side of her, with his hands on the worktable, he continued his exploration. "Hmm, yes, more."

Finally, he lifted his head and captured her mouth, wanting to keep up the slow assault, but the sheer intensity of the contact battered his control. Needing to hold her, he gathered her up into a full embrace.

Her arms went around his neck, drawing him in, urging him on. He'd always loved it when she accepted him like that. Widening his stance, he pressed the small of her back to bring her lower torso into his. Again, he groaned but didn't break the kiss. She settled her hips into him and stood on her toes. He parted her lips, darted inside her mouth, explored it. When her tongue met his, his body bucked into her.

It wasn't enough, though, and in one burst of sanity he realized nothing ever was, or would be, enough with this woman. Drawing back, he heard her whimper "No." He said, "Shh," as he grabbed her around the waist— not gently—and hiked her onto the bench. She opened her legs and he stepped between them. His gaze linked with hers, and the unadulterated lust he saw in her eyes matched his own.

Grasping the hem of her T-shirt, he drew it over her head and tossed it aside. Some black lacy thing bound her breasts and the tops swelled over it. "Oh, damn, oh, God, you're even more gorgeous now. More lush."

But before he could go further, she pulled at *his* shirt and dragged the thing up. He helped her get it over his head.

"Mmm," she said, and leaned forward. Her mouth moved over his pecs, kissed, then licked.

He grasped her arms. "Sweetheart, do you know what you're doing to me—what you've been doing to me since you came to town?"

Her fingers skimmed down his abs, flirted with the waistband of his shorts. Then, oh, man, they went lower and her whole palm pressed against his groin. "Mmm-hmm."

It was too much. He had to have more, so he pushed her back and reached for the front clasp of her bra.

Before he could free her, some kind of banging sounded behind him. "Hey, Luke, what's this hose…" The voice drifted off and Luke drew Jayne to him, to shield her from Jess.

But he was yanked away by the shoulder, jerked around, pushed back. Jess got a glimpse of Jayne, stepped between her and Luke, and dropped the still-running hose. "What the f… You bastard."

Before Luke could react, Jess bent low and went for him. Luke stumbled back and out of the shed. They both fell to the ground. Luke's head hit hard as he went down. He saw a blur of movement and then pain splintered through his jaw, spiraling outward to his whole face. Jess raised his fist again, but Jayne came into view and grabbed his arm.

"Jess, no! What are you doing?"

Suddenly, Jess's assault stopped. He looked up at Jayne, whom Luke could see was now fully clothed, and gulped in a breath. "Are you all right?"

"Of course I am." She tugged hard on his arm until he climbed off Luke and stood. "What are you doing?" she repeated.

"Don't you know what's going on here?" He studied her face. "Oh, no, you don't! You thought this was real."

"I…we…look, Jess, something just happened between me and Luke."

"Don't you know *why?*"

She shook her head.

Managing to turn to his side, Luke struggled to his feet, saw red drops on his chest and tasted copper in his mouth. His jaw hurt like hell.

Jess focused on him. "You son of a bitch. How dare you use her like this?"

Luke said, "Use her?"

And Jayne uttered, "Use me?" at the same time.

Jess's face softened. "Jaynie, Luke's making a move on you so Naomi and I will have a clear road to getting back together." Jess's eyes widened, then he sent a lethal glare to Luke. "Or are you planning to toy with her— which, by the way, you're very good at—then break her heart so she'll leave town?"

Vaguely, Jayne remembered Jess's comments about Luke's rep with women. And in New York, hadn't she always wondered what he saw in her?

"H-he's doing *that?*" Jayne whispered.

"The hell I am!" Luke's voice rose, but he didn't care.

"Oh, God." Jayne's hands clapped against her mouth.

"Oh, God, I didn't know…I never thought." She looked at him. "How *could* you?"

"I *didn't*," he said. "For God's sake, Jayne, I didn't." He nodded to the shed. "It was all real in there, just like before."

"Just like before?" Jess asked. "What do you mean?"

Luke started to answer when Jess glanced behind him. "Naomi? What are you doing here?"

Whirling around, Luke saw Jess's wife standing a few feet away. Her face was ashen and her hands fisted at her sides.

"I knew you were at church, so I came to talk to Jayne. I thought maybe…never mind." Her hands went to her hips. "I guess it's a good thing I did, isn't it, Jess? I got to witness your jealousy firsthand."

"No, Nay, you got it all wrong."

"Oh, yeah, sure, try to tell me what I saw with my own eyes didn't happen. You're a liar, Jess, and a fool." She turned on her heel and stalked away.

After a moment's hesitation, and a glance at Jayne, Jess went after his wife. Luke watched first Naomi, then Jess, round the corner of the house and disappear.

When they were alone, Jayne raised bleak eyes to him.

Pissed, Luke said, "Tell me you don't believe him."

Her look said she did.

"Damn it, Jayne, I still have feelings you. I never got over them."

She shook her head wildly. "I don't believe that."

"Why?"

"It doesn't matter." She started to walk away.

He grabbed her arm. "You're just going to run again, like you did before, aren't you?"

"Running away from you is a very good idea." She shook him off. "Leave me alone, Luke. I mean it."

Dumbfounded, he stared after her, wondering how the hell something so special had gone this far south.

CHAPTER EIGHT

JAYNE SAT at the desk in her bedroom in Eleanor's house, peering through the bay window that overlooked the gardens. It was eleven at night and darkness blanketed the flower beds. Still, their sweetness wafted up as if Mother Nature had sprayed a puff of her perfume just for Jayne. Usually, she took comfort in the evening beauty of outdoors. But not tonight.

In front of her was the official report she'd received today on the collapse of the walkway in the Coulter Gallery. Jess had been right to suspect the mistake had occurred in a change made after the original drawings had been completed. The fault did indeed lie in the steel rods that anchored the joists. Instead of one rod inserted in the middle of each beam, which she'd originally drawn into the design, she'd signed off on changing the order to two rods at either end, so the bolts didn't have to be threaded.

Now that she knew what the problem was, Jayne recalled the concession she'd made to the structural engineer, Paul Gerber, whom the gallery had hired.

"It'll save big bucks if we don't have to thread the rods." His tone was impatient, as usual.

"Cost isn't the only factor to consider," Jayne had told him.

"Hell, Jayne, you've said that about almost all the things that could be changed to save us some money."

Trying not to bristle, she said crisply, "My original plans work with the joists."

"Look, here's some research I did on the Web. I also called a couple of my colleagues, since I thought you'd balk again. Everybody agrees that if they're set right, the double rods will work."

She scanned the papers he handed her.

"So, what's the harm on this one?"

There didn't appear to be any. Two of the Web sites said multiple bolts would be *more* secure. And though Jayne had had a lot of run-ins with this guy, she wouldn't have conceded the point about the rods unless she'd thought it was safe. The research, combined with the fact that Gerber was a *structural* engineer and had the approval of others in his field, had convinced her.

So she'd given in on this one and the cost had been higher than she could have possibly imagined: her architectural career. Because, next to the official report, were two other mailings that had been forwarded to her.

The first and most damning was a report from the independent outfit she'd hired, confirming the board's conclusions. The double rods in the joists had not been able to handle the weight of the building.

Next was a certified letter from one of her clients confirming her fears about her professional reputation.

Due to the collapse of the Coulter Gallery walkway, the city of Phoenix, Arizona, is invoking the cancellation clause in our contract, which states if any detrimental event occurs to other projects designed by Logan Architects, we reserve

the right to nullify our agreement with the afore-
mentioned firm to design the Phoenix Convention
Center.

Logan Associates had the right to keep the one
hundred thousand dollar down payment, but Jayne had
no intention of doing that. She had some pride left.

"So," she said into the empty room, sipping a glass
of merlot, staring at the pieces of her broken life, "this
is how it's going to be."

She wished Jess was here. She wished she had a
girlfriend to call and talk to, like she'd had in Sally. But
most of all, she wished Luke's attentions on Sunday had
been genuine and he was with her to make her see
things in a different light, as he'd done before.

Everybody makes mistakes.

But Jess was gone. By Sunday night, he'd left town.
He'd come to tell her why. She'd been inconsolable
about the debacle with Luke but hid it from her friend
because he was in a worse state.

"I'm going away, Jaynie. I…" His hazel eyes had
moistened. "I keep screwing up. Naomi won't listen to
the truth, and I punched out my best friend. Something's wrong with me."

"No, Jess…."

He held up his hands. "I'm going to a monastery
Pastor Wilkins suggested." The reverend had been vol-
unteering at the Harmony site as part of the Riverdale
church contingent, and Jess had become friends with
him. "It's a silent retreat. I need to get my act together."

"I'm so sorry this caused you grief. I should just—"

"I'm not strong enough to fight with you about
staying. Promise me one thing."

"Anything, Jess. I'd do anything for you."

"Don't leave town while I'm gone."

"All right."

So she'd stayed and even gone to the Harmony Housing site to work. Where, shockingly, she'd encountered an angry Luke Corelli. *He'd* been angry. The gall of him, she'd thought initially.

He'd stood in the doorway of the trailer, hard hat in one hand, the thumb of his other hooked in his jeans belt loop. There was an inferno in his eyes, making them darker, almost liquid. "I'm surprised you showed up here today." Even his tone had been cut-glass cold. "I figured you'd be long gone by now, that you'd run again."

She lifted a brow, hoping her haughty expression would distance him. "I changed my mind."

He waved his hand to encompass the interior of the trailer. "Even though you'll have to work with me?" Shaking his head in disgust, he added, "Why would you want be around somebody you believe is such a scumbag?"

"I'm not afraid to see you. I made a mistake in judgment Sunday morning." It had to be more than that, she knew. Jayne had believed Jess automatically because she still couldn't trust men. After what had happened with Ben, she probably never would. "Let's forget it happened."

"A mistake in judgment? Is that what you're calling it? Lady, you're something else."

"What do you mean?"

"We were all over each other in that shed." He rubbed his neck. "I have the skid marks to prove it."

Mention of what Jayne had done to him and the quick peek she got at a dark bruise when his collar tugged back made her gasp.

"We were totally into each other. If Jess hadn't interrupted, you know what would have happened."

"Then it's a good thing he did."

Luke had approached her, circled the desk and dragged her up. "Goddamn you, how can you say that to me? After what we shared in that shed?"

"We shared nothing. You, on the other hand, are very good at manipulation."

"What about before? In New York?"

"It was a fling. The kind you're known for, Luke. Everybody in town is aware of that. Even Jess said so."

His face turned stone-cold and he let go of her so fast she stumbled backward. "Are you still unsure of yourself as a woman? I thought you got past that with me." The last had come out hoarse.

He was right about the latter. With Luke she'd begun to feel sexy, feminine again. Then the problem with her firm had happened, she'd panicked, and denied all of it to herself.

She hadn't known what to say. When she remained silent, he spit out, "Forget it. Maybe you're not worth it." Then he walked out.

Even today, forty-eight hours later, she'd had no retort for him. But she did have a niggling suspicion that she'd overreacted. His anger in the office had been so real, so genuine. And something else. When he got close, she could see in his eyes that he'd been hurt, hear the faint traces of it underlying his tone.

She glanced down at the white silk robe she wore over a matching nightgown that hid a few marks of her own. And she admitted to herself that Luke was right.

After her experience with Ben, she had no confidence in herself as a woman.

SWINGING HIS RACKET back, Luke swooped down on the ball a few inches from the floor and slapped it forward. The little blue sphere slammed into the front wall and came back to hit Belle in the arm.

"Damn it, Luke, take it easy."

"Look, you're no cream puff out here either. You've been whacking up a storm."

"Shut up and serve."

He didn't take it easy on her. Instead, he smashed the next shot right below the line, so the ball sliced toward her, fast and low. Belle dived for it and missed, skidding across the floor on her forearms. Ouch! That had to hurt. Dropping his racket, he hustled over to her.

"You okay?"

She rolled over on her back and he saw brush burns on her skin.

"Hell." He jogged to the side to retrieve water and a towel from his bag. When he returned, he hunched in front of her and started to treat the scrapes. She was sitting up now.

He pressed the cold cloth on her.

"That hurts."

"Hush. This'll make it feel better in a minute."

She hissed in reaction to his ministrations. She'd been in a snit since they met at the gym a half hour ago, and he assumed it was because of Kenny's incident with the police and dealing with a teenager who was grounded for a month. For his part, Luke had played like a maniac because he was furious at Jayne. And Jess. No, the thing with Jess hurt. He was mad as hell at Jayne.

"We're a pair," he said as he blotted the worst of the

bruises. Sweat was dripping off his face and Belle's shirt was soaked through.

"You wanna go first?"

"No, you go. It's Kenny, right?"

"Actually, it's Nick."

Luke's head snapped up. Belle and Nick were the happiest couple he knew. She was a nurse, he was a doctor. They'd been married eighteen years and the depth of their feelings for each other was obvious to everyone around them. But today Luke saw concern in her dark eyes, and that worried him. "What about Nick?"

"We're fighting over our son."

"Is that all?"

"It's enough. He thinks I'm too hard on Kenny. He said if I hadn't forbidden him to hang out with those kids, he probably wouldn't have rebelled and gone out with them to drink."

"Is that true?"

"No, I think Kenny was just disobeying his parents."

"This doesn't sound too serious, sweetie."

"Serious enough for me to refuse to have sex with my husband and ergo, we're sleeping in separate rooms."

"Wow. I'm sorry."

Picking up her racket, she banged the edge of it on the floor. "Nick's under stress at the hospital, and I realize that. His job's tough. But he shouldn't take it out on me."

"I know."

She nodded to the towel, which he'd kept wetting and applying to her arm. "I'm good."

Leaning against the wall, he indicated the court. "We're done for today."

"We should be. We're killing each other." She reached out and squeezed his hand. "What's going on with you?"

"I can't tell you, Belle."

His sister frowned. "Why? We talk about everything."

"I wish I could, because I need somebody to hash this out with. But you're biased."

A very long pause. "It's about Jayne Logan."

"I'm not going into it."

"You don't have to." He glanced over at Belle, who was staring ahead. "Naomi told me."

"Damn it."

Again, Belle was quiet for a long time. Then she said, "I'll be fair. My first concern is you. What happened?"

He had to get this out and, despite what he'd said about her bias, he trusted no one more than the woman beside him. "There's something you don't know about me and Jayne."

"What?"

"I, um, knew her in New York."

"Yeah, Jess asked you to get her in with Madison Conglomerates."

"I got involved with her there."

"Define *involved*."

"She calls it a fling." He shook his head. "But it was more to me. I fell for her, big-time."

"Really? I can't believe it. Women always chased you, not the other way around."

"First time for everything, I guess."

"What happened?"

"She ditched me without saying goodbye. Left because of a scandal at the architectural firm where she worked."

Belle waited.

"I thought I was over it. Hell, all that happened

twelve years ago and I've certainly gone on with my life. Then she came to town, and I started remembering things. It led to what happened yesterday."

He could still see Jayne hosing him down, racing to the shed, and laughing in the why-bother black bra.

"Jess found you and got jealous."

"No, I don't think so." He told Belle of Jess's accusations. "He freakin' punched me."

"I'm sorry, Luke. I know how you've depended on his friendship since Timmy died." She leaned into him and slid her arm through his. "What are you going to do about all this?"

"I have no idea." Just recounting Jayne's accusations infuriated him all over again. "Belle, tell me the truth. If I did pursue a relationship with her, could you ever accept her?"

"I'd try. Are you going to do it?"

"I don't know." How could he ever deal with the fact that Jayne believed he was a man without integrity? "I just don't know."

THE SUN BEAT DOWN on Jayne's head as she perched on the roof and anchored her feet on the section that was secure. Several pairs of workers were hammering plywood into place. A few feet away, Luke was nailing down a big board of it, and she worried about the precarious nature of his position. Hell, she'd been obsessed with him all week.

Come with me, he'd barked just an hour ago. *We don't have enough volunteers and I need somebody to feed me nails.*

She would have balked, but they *were* short of help, and he'd been so mean all week she didn't want to cross him. Oh, all right, she admitted as she stared over at him, his head bent, the brim of his Yankees cap pulled down. She wanted to be with him. He looked like a million bucks up here, shirtless, wearing a tool belt. And every time she handed him nails and their hands brushed, the electricity between them sizzled. She was afraid that, now that he'd touched her again, she wouldn't be able to forget what they had been like together.

They worked for an hour with the hot rays bouncing off the brown shingles mercilessly. She'd sweated through her Harmony Housing T-shirt, and the jeans she wore were sticking to her, never mind her feet swelling inside her work boots. She also felt a headache coming on and wished she'd brought medicine with her to the site.

When Luke deigned to look at her, he swore. "Don't you have enough sense to use sunscreen? Your nose is burning."

"I didn't know I'd be exposed this long."

"Go on down and put some on."

She glanced at her watch. "It's almost lunchtime. Let's finish this section and then stop for a while."

Something hit her in the chest.

"What?" She saw Luke's ball cap had landed on her. "I don't want to wear your hat."

"You didn't seem to mind wearing one of mine on Sunday." She could practically see anger bubbling inside him as she tossed the hat back and he jerked it on. "And no matter what you say, you didn't mind a lot of things that morning."

"Shut up."

"Excuse me?"

"I said shut up. I don't want to talk about this."

He swore under his breath and, with the force of an anvil hitting steel, hammered another nail. When she went to give him more, he grabbed her fingers. Nails fell, pinging on the wood, and slid off the roof. "Don't tell me you don't remember what it was like to have my hands on you again." He nodded to her breasts. "All over you. You wanted it, babe."

"I never said I didn't want it."

"Oh, wait, I forgot. You said you didn't believe it was real. How in the holy hell could you think I faked that response to you? Especially after what we shared in New York?"

"You said it was because I didn't have any confidence in myself as a woman." Her tone came off hurt instead of nasty, like she meant it.

He stopped nailing and sat back on his haunches. "I was mad."

"Maybe you were right."

His brow furrowed and she noticed lines of fatigue around his eyes and mouth. "About what?"

"I don't have much confidence in myself as a woman."

"You were getting over that, Jayne, with me."

"I thought so. But when I left you, any progress I made dissipated."

"That's just plain nuts."

When she didn't say more, he turned and sat down on the section of the roof he'd finished, then slid closer to her. From his tool belt he took out a bottle of water, sipped from the thing and handed it to her. She took a swig without realizing the intimacy of the gesture until she gave it back to him.

"Honey, please." He grasped her hand. "Believe that I was sincere in that shed."

"I'd like—"

"Hey, Jayne!" The call came from the ground, irritating her. Suddenly she wanted to have this conversation with Luke. She wanted to examine her feelings and motives, along with his. But one of the women carpenters was standing below, peering up at them and shading her eyes with her hands.

"What, Carla?" Jayne yelled down.

"There's somebody here for you." She chuckled. "He looks like Jude Law."

Oh, dear Lord.

Luke said, "Who's…Jayne, are you all right?"

Open mouthed, her heart beating like a drum, she shook her head as she watched a man come toward the house.

His stride was still the same…long and graceful, like a runner's.

His tan lightweight suit stretched across shoulders that had once been safe and comforting.

His hair was still thick and run-your-fingers-through-it appealing.

All these details told her one thing.

"What's wrong?" Luke asked. "You're trembling."

She swallowed hard and stared down at the ground.

"Who's that?"

"D-Ben Scarborough."

"The Ben from college? The one who turned on you and Jess?"

"Yes." She glanced over at Luke and saw the surprise on his face. "The one who made me lose that confidence we were just talking about."

HE FELT LIKE a teenager following his girl around, but nonetheless, when Jayne climbed down the ladder and the asshole who'd betrayed her had the gall to envelop her in a warm hug, Luke seemed to turn into a juvenile. He hustled down the rungs, too, and stood behind her when he reached the ground.

"Ben?" she asked, "What are you *doing* here?"

"I'm looking for you." The guy's tone was as smooth as the silk tie he wore. "I went to Jess's house and Eleanor told me you were working here, but Jess was out of town."

"I...why?"

Scarborough glanced behind her. "Hi, I'm Ben Scarborough."

Stepping to Jayne's side, Luke moved in close. "Got a lot of nerve showing up here, don't you, Scarborough?"

The guy recoiled.

"This is Luke Corelli—Jess's best friend."

At least the man had the grace to flush. "Oh, well then, his...attitude makes sense."

"You didn't answer the lady's question."

Now annoyance showed in his *Jude Law* baby blues. Hell, why couldn't the guy look like Woody Allen? "Is there somewhere we can talk, Jayne?"

"You're kidding, right? I don't want to talk to you. How could you even think I would?"

With a quick glance at Luke, he said, "I thought maybe you'd remember what we had together and hear me out."

"You betrayed me and I've never forgotten that, Ben. Never."

Good for her, Luke thought.

"There are some things you don't know. Some things I never told you. Just give me a chance to say them aloud, then if you want me to, I'll leave." He held up a bag Luke hadn't noticed he was holding. "I brought your favorite raisin bagels and strawberry cream cheese."

"I haven't had those in ages."

Jeez, was she buying this crap?

Time for some intervention. "Get out of here, Scarborough. She said she doesn't want to see you."

Scarborough gave her a pleading look.

"Oh, all right. There's a picnic table in some trees out there." She glanced over at Luke. He wished she was angry or bitter, but instead she looked scared.

Which was why, when she and Ben headed to the rear of the lot, Luke grabbed some coffee and stood by a tree a discreet distance away to watch what was going on. For about ten minutes, Jayne looked like she was giving Scarborough hell and he was doing his best to grovel. But when Jayne went all soft and feminine on him, Luke threw away the cup and charged to the other side of the trees behind the picnic table, where he was hidden from their view but could hear their conversation.

Scarborough was talking. "I've never forgiven myself for what I did to you and Jess in college. I tried to forget it and go on with my life. I got married, had two kids, then divorced, but everything seemed tainted. I need your forgiveness, I guess."

"All right. You have it. You can go now."

Some rustling. Probably getting out her *favorite* bagel.

"Here, have one of these. There's more I want to say. Let me explain the other reason I came here."

"All right, explain."

"News of the collapse made it through the architectural grapevine. I was shocked and concerned. So I followed up with some connections I have, and when I found out the cause—that you were at fault—I thought I might be able to do something. So I came here."

"How did you know I'd be in Riverdale, anyway?"

"I called your father. He told me where you went."

"Why would he do that? He hated you after you blamed me and Jess for cheating."

"It's a long story. I'd rather not talk about it here, J.J."

J.J.? What the hell?

"Don't call me that."

"It's how I think of you—that unbelievably smart but shy girl in college."

"I'm not that girl anymore, Ben."

"No, you're a beautiful woman." His voice pitched lower, sexy and lover like.

Huh! Luke knew how to do that, too.

"Stop it!"

"I'm sorry. It's just that being with you, this close to you, brings something different out in me."

Join the club, buddy.

"Did you come to gloat?"

Luke could picture Jayne staring at Scarborough, waiting until he answered her question.

"No, of course not. I'm guessing you need friends right now. I'm here to make amends with Jess, too. I thought I might do that by helping you."

"Even if I'd let you, what could you possibly do, Ben?"

"I have a firm in Manhattan. Scarborough Associates. I'm the head architect. It's very successful."

The guy was so modest.

"I want you to come to New York and work with me."

"What?"

"I'm offering you a job."

"I don't know if I'll get to keep my architecture license."

"Then we'll find something else for you to do. It's a huge firm. You can have your pick of projects to consult on."

"I don't know what to say."

Hell, she couldn't be considering this, could she?

Then Luke remembered the things Jess had told him about the two of them: Jayne had never had a serious boyfriend before Ben. She fell head over heels for the guy. They were talking about getting married. And just now, she'd confessed the power Scarborough had over her by depriving her of her confidence as a woman.

"This is too much to take in," Jayne was saying.

"I know. I'm staying a few days so we can talk it through."

I'll just bet you are.

"Have dinner with me tonight. I'm checked in at the Baron Steuben. They've got a good dining room."

And hotel rooms, where Luke knew Scarborough would try to lure *J.J.*

Over Luke's dead body.

Tossing the cup aside, Luke noisily circled the trees and made his presence known.

"Luke?" Jayne regarded him suspiciously. "What are you doing…?" She glanced at the direction he'd come from. "Were you eavesdropping on us?"

He pushed back the bill of his ball cap and put his hands on his hips. "Yeah, I was. And a good thing, too. You're really buying this crap, aren't you?"

"WHAT WERE YOU thinking?" Jayne had walked Ben to his car and then made a beeline back to Luke.

People were staring at them, but they were out of earshot.

"Damn it, Luke."

"I was watching out for you." He was wearing his T-shirt now, and had ditched the tool belt. "Jess is out of town, so somebody's got to do it."

"I can take care of myself."

"Oh, yeah, you were doing a great job of it, *J.J.*" He scowled. "What the hell does that stand for, anyway?"

"Jayne Jordan, my mother's maiden name." She blew out a breath, rustling the damp bangs on her forehead. "Luke, you're avoiding my question. Why would you interfere like this?"

"Because I have a right."

"A *right?*"

"Yeah." He glanced behind her and must have seen they'd gathered an audience. "Hell." Taking her by the arm, he practically dragged her into the trailer and slammed the door.

"Stop manhandling me!" She shook him off and rounded on him. "You have *no* rights with me. Why would you think you do?"

His eyes narrowed; he moved in fast and yanked on the neckline of the shirt she wore. "This gives me the right."

Jayne looked down. The swell of her breasts still bore evidence of his ardor and suddenly her mind was propelled back into the shed when Luke had his mouth on her, nipping and soothing.

She jerked away. "No, I won't let you do this. Not again. You have no claim to me, and if I choose to forgive Ben—hell, if I choose to sleep with him—it's my decision."

"You'd *sleep* with him?"

Why couldn't he have lashed out in anger again? Instead, the words, uttered with gentle horror, made her take in a sharp breath.

Dear God, had he really been involved in the shed? Had he really meant what he said?

CHAPTER NINE

HUMILIATED BEYOND BELIEF, Luke yanked up the covers on Elise's bed, wishing he could crawl under them instead.

"I…I'm sorry. I don't know why…"

He let the words trail off because he did indeed know why he couldn't make love with Elise, and he hated lying to her face.

"It's all right, Luke. This happens."

For a moment, he stared at the incredibly beautiful woman next to him, wrapped in sheets that matched her blue eyes. "Not to me."

Her smile was comforting. "There's always a first time."

"So they say." He whipped back the covers and dragged on his boxers. "I'm going to get a drink. Want something?"

"A glass of red wine would be nice." She grabbed his hand as he passed her and kissed it. "Luke, honestly, no big deal."

Feeling like a complete hypocrite, he took his time finding his way through the condo. It was a pretty little thing, a lot like Elise herself. He was mad as hell that he'd been unable to perform and felt like a total jerk for putting Elise in this awkward position.

Unfortunately, he knew what the problem was.

The liquor cabinet sat against a wall, a few feet away from the set of tapestry couches. Drawing out the Johnny Walker, he poured a hefty amount, crossed to the window and looked out at the wooded yard. He wasn't ready to go back upstairs yet. And he knew Elise would give him time. She was a nice person as well as a knockout.

But, Luke admitted in the dim light of the night, he didn't want her, as evidenced by his lack of performance. Nope, he wanted Jayne Logan with a passion that shocked him. And he'd been foolish and selfish to call Elise in the first place, to hope she could make him forget all about the woman who was driving him absolutely crazy. Damn it, when had he become so self-centered?

Gimme a break, Timmy had said once when he'd asked his friend that question. *You've always been like this. You had five mothers and were the center of attention all your life. I hate you for it, buddy.* Then Timmy had socked him in the arm, taking the sting out of his words with his next statement. *But you've got a good heart and you'd give anybody the shirt off your back.*

Timmy's observation had been right on target. But Luke had thought, with his friend's death, he'd changed. Images of that time crept into his mind, images he had to forcefully keep at bay. It was hard. As always, when he was upset, Luke would return to that dark place. "Don't do it," he ordered himself.

The lesser of two evils was to think about Jayne. Jayne, who right now was doing what? He glanced at his watch. Dinner at the Baron Steuben would be over by now. Had they gone back to Scarborough's room?

I'll sleep with him if I want.

She'd said those words to him, so he wasn't imagining things. She could very well be in the guy's bed right now, letting him give her back some of that confidence he stole from her when she was barely out of her teens. And why the hell shouldn't she? She owed Luke nothing, contrary to what he'd told her earlier. After all, it had been twelve freaking years since they'd been together, and he'd never tried to contact her.

But, damn it all, he knew he'd gone a long way in restoring her confidence when they were together in New York, and he should be the one to bring it to fruition now. Belle had told him once there was nothing like knowing you pleased a man in bed. Luke wanted to bathe Jayne in sensual experience after sensual experience, so she'd never doubt herself again.

Oh, sure! he thought glancing down at his groin. *Now you come to attention. With only* thoughts *of Jayne.* "Where were you earlier, boy?"

One thing was clear. Luke wasn't being fair to Elise. Waiting a bit for his body to calm down, he poured Elise her favorite Shiraz and headed upstairs.

She was still in bed, staring out the window at the moon. The faint trace of her perfume and lotions hung in the air. "You okay?" she asked when he entered the room and she accepted the wine from him.

Dropping down on her side of the mattress, he faced her—and the issue—squarely. "We have to talk."

"Uh-oh. Nothing good ever follows those words."

"This will be good for you."

She arched a brow.

"I don't think we should see each other for a while."

"Luke, if it's about this—" she patted the bed "—I understand."

"It is about that, in a way."

"What do you mean?"

"I couldn't do anything with you tonight because I've been—" he wanted to be delicate "—caught up in things with someone else. Another woman."

"Ah." She sipped the Shiraz, looked at him pointedly. "Jayne Logan."

He frowned. "How would you know that?"

"Methinks the gentleman doth protest too much."

"At the party?"

"And other times. You don't realize how much you talk about her, in negative terms, but still she seems to have gotten…inside you." She added, "Rather quickly."

"I used to know her in New York."

"Really?"

"Yeah, it didn't work out. It won't this time, either."

She waited a beat. "Maybe you should try again."

"You're being pretty understanding."

"Don't get me wrong. I was looking forward to where this was going between us. But I don't want you, Luke, if you want someone else. Truthfully, I've been down that road once and don't intend to travel it again." She traced her finger around the rim of the wineglass. "However, if you decide that your feelings for her weren't what you thought, that you're over her, and I'm still free, maybe we can try again."

She was letting him off the hook, which he didn't deserve, and he sighed as he stared at her. Why couldn't he have fallen for this understanding, generous woman instead of a prickly, stubborn, withholding one like Jayne—who right now might be making love to another man?

JAYNE SAT in a booth at the bar of the Baron Steuben sipping her second glass of wine that night, listening to a musician play the piano in the corner and staring at a man she'd once adored. As an adult, he was even more attractive than he'd been as a boy with that perfectly cut hair, those powerful masculine hands and blue eyes she used to get lost in.

"What are you thinking?" he asked.

"How handsome you are."

He seemed startled. "Thanks. And I return the compliment." He nodded to the dress she'd worn to Eleanor's party. "You're lovely tonight."

You'd better fix that thing, Luke had said when the bodice had slipped after she'd fallen off the chair. His eyes had been hot.

Go away, she thought for the hundredth time that night.

"Jayne, I didn't want to ruin dinner, but I was hoping if I told you more about what happened in college, it might make your decision to let me help you easier."

Her heart started to beat fast. "It's still painful for me to talk about that time in my life."

"I'm sure it is. But there are some things you don't know."

Cocking her head, she sensed something important was coming. "I thought we shared everything back then."

"Not this." He sipped his wine and glanced away. "My dad lost his job right before our junior year because he was drinking."

"Why didn't you tell me?"

"I was afraid to. You came from a successful family. I didn't want you to know you were paired up with the son of a drunk."

"I wouldn't have judged you."

"Maybe not, but your father would have. He had me investigated."

She gripped the stem of her glass. *"What?"*

"After I met him, he hired a private detective to find out about me and my family. Some people in my hometown told me they'd been contacted."

Now that she thought about it, Jayne recalled taking Ben to New York, and how her father had grilled him about his background. When he realized they were serious, he must have hired a private investigator to find out more about Ben.

"Damn him. My father had no right."

"He was protecting his daughter." A sad smile crossed Ben's lips. "Now that I have two of my own, I understand that. In any case, I had nothing to hide then. My father's drinking escalated fast. Before I knew it, he was in A.A. and unemployed."

Concern was replaced by pique. "You should have told me this, Ben. I would have stood by you, helped you through it."

"I was afraid I'd lose you."

"Instead, you betrayed me?"

Briefly, he closed his eyes and took a deep breath. "I was on a scholarship. If I'd admitted we cut corners in our research, Sally and I would have gotten the F and I would have lost my chance to finish college."

She'd known about the scholarship, of course, but had never put that particular spin on things. It didn't, however, excuse what they'd done.

"After we lied and you and Jess got blamed, I decided I couldn't go through with the deception and headed back to the house to confess everything. But before I got there, my mother called and asked me to come home. Dad had gotten a DWI and all hell had broken loose." He ran a hand through his hair. "Afterward, I chickened out again."

"How does Sally fit into all this?"

"She was scared, too. You know she was never as strong as you and Jess. Neither was I, for that matter. But none of this excuses us. What we did was unconscionable. I can't tell you how happy I was when you and Jess were exonerated."

"Cornell asked me to come back as a guest lecturer." And she'd taken pleasure in gloating to the very professors who hadn't recommended her to a top firm in the field.

What would they be thinking now?

"Jayne?"

"I'm glad you told me. It puts everything in perspective."

Reaching across the table, he took her hand. The connection felt familiar and strange at the same time. "For what it's worth, I missed you like I'd miss my right arm. I watched you from afar—getting out of the mess I created, graduating summa cum laude. Starting your firm."

"What about your wife and family?"

"Sara never knew what I did in college. Though I'm not sure I was a very good husband. She divorced me because I worked too much and neglected her. What a cliché."

"I'm sorry for you, Ben."

"Are you?"

"Yes. But I admire you for coming here to explain, and I appreciate it." She did. Her heart felt lighter.

"I want to tell this all to Jess, too."

"That would be good. He gets home tomorrow."

Ben gave her the tender smile she remembered from college when they *made up* after a fight. "Thanks for listening, J.J. So, what do you say? Want to leave Riverdale now and work for me?"

"Even before I receive the final decision about my license?"

"Yes. I told you, there are plenty of jobs for you to do." That smile broadened. "And maybe we can see if there's still something between us."

Jayne sat back in the chair. This was a great offer professionally. She wasn't likely to get many, even if she did retain her license. Staring over at the man she'd once loved, she realized with remarkable clarity that she *had* been woman enough for him. And, now, maybe they could go back to what they'd once had together.

If that was what she really wanted.

Was it?

LUKE PROWLED around his house imagining all sorts of scenarios for what was going on between Jayne and Ben. At least he was able to keep himself from barging over to the Baron Steuben and dragging Jayne out by the hair. That would have gone over really big!

Instead, since he'd arrived home from Elise's two hours ago, he'd fixed a leaky pipe, torn up the carpet in the den where he was planning to install hardwood floors and watered the damn plants his sisters insisted he keep around.

He'd taken a scalding shower and dressed in navy Gap pajama bottoms, and still wasn't tired. The doorbell rang while he was watching an old Western in bed. He was glad for the distraction until he checked the bedside clock and saw it was midnight. A visitor this late was not good news. Fear that something had happened to someone in his family made his heart race as he pounded downstairs and whipped open the door.

He was so relieved—and stunned—to find Jayne on his porch he could barely breathe. Finally he was able to utter, "This is a surprise."

"Is it?"

"Yeah. You had a date tonight."

"I did."

He scowled when he noticed what she was wearing. "Dressed up for him, huh?"

"Well, you know how fragile my feminine ego is."

He couldn't decipher her mood, so he waited.

"Can I come in?"

"I guess." He stepped aside and she walked into the foyer. As she passed him, she scraped her nails over his bare chest. "Aren't you cold?"

"You gotta be kidding me."

A Mata Hari smile crossed her lips. What was she up to?

Instead of telling him, she said, "Nice house."

"It's getting there."

"I wouldn't have figured you for a fixer-upper. Your place in New York was sleek and modern."

"How'd you know where to find me?"

"Jess drove by here once to show me. I love the exterior. It's a good…skin for the house."

That was exactly what he'd thought.

"He said you redid the siding when you bought it."

"I did." Why the hell was she talking about his house?

She sashayed to the entrance of the living room and he caught sight of the same sexy sandals she'd worn the night of the party. Ones that made her legs look long and luscious. "Oh, that fireplace. It has to be original."

Despite his confusion, and distraction, he smiled at the fieldstone that he'd cleaned and polished a hundred times until it shone. He watched her stroll around the area, run her hand over the chocolate leather couches and study his prints on the wall. "I like this room."

"I'm glad it meets with your approval."

Glancing over at him, she raised her brows. "Grumpy tonight, aren't you?"

"Yeah, well, I got reason."

"You do?"

He cocked his head. "You tell me. What happened with Scarborough?"

"A lot." Her expression became sober. "He had an explanation for why he did what he did to Jess and me."

"It can't possibly be good enough."

"It was. I'll tell you about it sometime."

"I can't wait." His tone was sarcastic. He moved farther into the room and folded his arms over his chest. "What about the job offer?"

"Ah, now that's why I came here." She faced him and licked her lips, newly covered with raisin-colored gloss. "I wanted your opinion. Should I take Ben's offer, Luke?"

"What do you mean?"

"Do you think I should take the job and move to New York? It'd make the situation between Jess and Naomi better."

Why was she asking him that? And what should he say? "No, you shouldn't take it. You shouldn't go to New York."

Her smile intensified. "Why not?"

"You know why not."

"Tell me."

He covered the distance between them and grasped her arms. The feel of her under his hands made his words come out even more forcefully. "I want you to stay in Riverdale. With me. What happened in the shed was real and, what's more, I've never really gotten over you."

"Hmm." She ran her hands up his bare skin, leaned in and sniffed his chest. "Luke, I'd like to see more of the house."

"What?" She was scrambling his brains. "What part?"

"Your bedroom." She stood on tiptoe and kissed his lips lightly. "Take me upstairs."

His answer was to lean over, slide an arm under her legs and the other around her back and scoop her up. "Thank God" was all he said as he cuddled her to his chest and took the steps two at a time.

JAYNE WAS UNABLE to think, unable to take in her surroundings as Luke gently placed her on his lake of a bed. He sat down next to her and she reached for him. "Not so fast," he whispered. "I'm going to look my fill. Touch my fill."

"I guess you can do that."

Gently he traced her mouth with a fingertip. When she got the chance, she nipped at it.

"Careful there. We don't want to rush this."

He outlined her eyebrows and her jaw. Closing her eyes, she savored his touch. This time, she felt secure in the knowledge that what they were doing came from his heart. Otherwise, he would have encouraged her to go with Ben.

"I was insanely jealous tonight," he said as he kissed

his way over her collarbone from one shoulder to another. His hair brushed her face and she threaded her fingers through it at the nape.

"Hmm."

"I hated the thought of him touching you."

A hesitation. Then, "He didn't, Luke."

"Good." He drew back and brushed her cheek with his knuckles. She could smell the soap from his shower. "I told Elise tonight I couldn't see her anymore. Because of you."

"Ah."

Lowering his head, he took her mouth. Possessed it. Explored the inside. She was breathing hard when he drew back. "So we're square, right?"

She ran her hands over his shoulders. "Uh-huh. Now, shut up, and get with the program."

"Aren't you the romantic?"

"How's this—I want your hands on me, everywhere. I want your mouth, too."

"A lot better." Leaning over, he whispered in her ear, "I want to be inside you, Jayne. Deep, deep inside you."

"Oh, God." Her lower body squirmed at his words.

He took the opportunity to grasp the bodice of her dress and draw it down to her waist. She was totally exposed to him. Never unlocking their gazes, he cupped both breasts. Gently kneaded. Again her eyes closed, savoring the moment. He bent his head and began to suckle on a nipple. A bolt of lust shot through her, making her buck. His hands became more urgent, roaming her hot flesh with need.

"Lift up," he whispered, and she raised her hips so he could whisk the dress off. He shook his head at the only thing she was wearing…a naughty red thong. His big hands weren't so gentle when he dragged the scrap of lace off her.

She was bare to him, but instead of being unsure, she basked in his approval—the same approval she'd seen in his eyes years ago and forgotten about.

"You are so lovely, even more than before. You take my breath away."

"I want to be, for you." She tugged at the drawstring of his pajama bottoms. "Return the favor."

His grin was arrogant; he was a man who knew the strength of his own virility. "Whatever you want." Standing, he dropped his pants. An impressive erection nestled in the curls that matched the hair on his head. His abs were tight, his hips narrow. He was different too, older, but well toned and muscular.

Jayne grasped him boldly. Now, *his* eyes closed, and his hands fisted at his sides. He let her massage him for a few seconds, then drew her away. "Can't do this, sweetheart."

"Why? You got to touch me."

"You know damn well why." He slid open the drawer, dragged out a condom and offered it to her. "But you can do the honors."

"My pleasure."

"Not yet, darlin'. Not yet."

ALL TEASING VANISHED as soon as Luke covered her body with his. It felt so good, he was afraid he was going to come right there and then. He tried to control himself, but he couldn't, his willpower slipping away by degrees.

"Come inside me, Luke," she whispered as if she knew. "I'm ready, too."

He did, with a thrust that was hard and fierce.

"Ohhh…"

"Did I hurt you?"

"No—" He moved inside her. "That feels…" She grabbed his shoulders. "Oh, Luke."

When he realized how close she was, he pushed harder, faster, until he felt her clench around him and her spasms begin.

He wanted to prolong this, but he couldn't, and he began to pound into her. Too soon, pleasure burst through him, exploded in his brain, and he erupted inside her.

Jayne opened her eyes, felt his weight, heard his labored breathing and realized his face was buried in her neck.

She cradled his head; he lifted it a minute later. No lines marring his mouth or forehead now, and he was smiling. "You all right?"

"Of course." She ran her fingertips over his scratchy jaw. "It was wonderful. Even better than I remembered."

"Glad to hear it. I lost consciousness there at the end."

"Then it was good?"

"Any more good and I'd be dead. You still pack quite a punch, Jayne Logan."

"So do you, Luke Corelli."

His smile was a little boyish. "I wanted it to last longer."

"Next time."

Rolling to his side, he quipped, "Give me a minute."

A chuckle escaped her as she moved into him, nestling her head in the crook of his arm. Absently he brushed her hair. She did the same to his chest.

He broke the silence. "What happened?"

She could pretend to misunderstand, tease, but she didn't. "I thought about it all week and listened to what you said in the trailer. I realized I had a knee-jerk reaction to Jess's accusations. Then you acted like such an idiot at the site when Ben came, I figured you were sincere in the shed."

"I was." He kissed her head.

"I'm glad." She sat up a bit and propped her forearms on his chest. "When Ben implied we might pick up where we left off, I knew I didn't want that. I wanted you."

"I want more than *this*."

"You said you needed a minute."

He kissed her nose. "I don't mean *that*."

"What do you want, Luke?" she asked directly.

"To see where this goes between us. I want you to stay in town and agree to pursue an exclusive relationship with me."

"All right, I will. But things are still a mess with me. It's not going to be a cakewalk."

"Well, since I'm so easygoing, I should be a good foil."

"Yeah, right."

"I'll help you through it, sweetheart."

"Okay." Again, she laid her head on his chest, the gesture tender and meaningful. And she told him the whole story of Ben and what had happened. He simply smoothed down her hair and listened.

When she finished, he asked, "So you forgive him?"

"Uh-huh. I hope Jess does, too." She waited, then asked him something she'd wanted to know since she'd come back to Riverdale and found him here. "Luke, tell me about your life for the last twelve years. Why haven't you ever married?"

THIS WAS GOING to be hard to talk about, but he'd try, for Jayne and the sake of their relationship. "After you left, I was shocked by how much I missed you."

"I wouldn't have guessed that."

"Well, I did."

"Didn't you date anyone else?"

"Yes. I got involved with a woman in New York about six months later." He shrugged. "It took me a long time to figure out it was a rebound relationship. After we got engaged and I asked her to come to Riverdale with me, I was relieved when she said no."

"Why?"

"I guess you were still in my blood, even then. Like I said, I missed you." He kissed her bare shoulder. "A lot."

"I missed you, too, though I told myself I didn't."

"Anyway, as I said the other night, Timmy was on the skids and I hadn't realized it was so bad. But instead of forgetting about you and helping him, I was a bastard to live with. I threw myself into my work. Ignored warning signs, like I told you the night of Eleanor's party. Then, when Timmy died and I came here, I could never establish a relationship that lasted."

"Because you felt guilty about Timmy?"

"Or because I was in an emotional coma. Hell, who knows? Maybe after I lost Timmy I was afraid to get too close to *anybody* again. It wasn't until you came to town that I admitted how much I'd cared about *you*." He was quiet for a few moments. "That's probably a better explanation of why I never got married."

"I…I'm flattered."

"You should be."

"Ah, I love your modesty."

He kissed her hard. "So that's my story. What about you? Are all the guys in California blind?"

She chuckled, then sobered. "I don't even know where to begin. After what happened with Ben, I was terrified of having a relationship. Then you came along, and when my feelings for you intensified, I panicked. I grew up emotionally stunted, Luke. Not encouraged to care about people like you do. It's one of the things that I loved most about you and that scared me at the same time." She sighed heavily. "It's why I left without talking to you first. I knew you could convince me to stay, and I wasn't ready to take any more risks."

"I knew you were upset about the bind your firm was in."

"Yeah, it wasn't like the incident at Cornell, but I worked on the project in question and was afraid they'd implicate me somehow."

"That's understandable, sweetheart."

She looked up at him. "It's so ironic. I've been obsessed about unfair allegations my entire adult life, and what do I do? I make a mistake and get a fair one." She swallowed hard. "I still can't believe it."

"Let's make a deal. We'll try to let the past go, try not to blame ourselves for mistakes we've made."

"Can you do that about Timmy?"

"I can try."

"Then so can I. It's a deal."

After a while, he could feel his body let go of its tension. "What about our other deal?"

"What?" she murmured against his chest.

"To make love slow, to take our time?"

"Hmm, I can't renege on a deal."

He flipped her over. Before he touched her, he whispered, "Thanks, Jayne. For being so honest."

She just smiled.

And continued to smile for the next hour.

So did Luke.

CHAPTER TEN

JAYNE WHIPPED off the covers and swung her feet to the floor. From the other side of the bed, an arm snaked around her waist, holding her in place. "Not so fast." Luke's voice was morning husky.

She glanced over her shoulder and smiled at the sight of him. His eyes were still closed, his head buried in the pillows, his bare back wide and tanned.

"I have to go."

"No way," he mumbled and tightened his grasp. "More sleep. It's Saturday."

She took a second to smooth down his dark hair, run her fingers over his beard-scratchy jaw. She never thought she'd be with him again like this, hadn't admitted how much she missed it, but now her feelings surfaced full force. "I have to get back to Eleanor's. It's ten, and Jess is due home this morning."

Burying his face further, Luke said, "I'll come."

"Um, no, you can't. Ben's meeting me there at eleven."

Luke's eyes snapped open. "The hell he is."

She kissed his cheek. "I told him last night I didn't want a relationship with him. But Jessie might, and I said I'd be there when Ben talks to him that there's someone else in my life."

Rolling to his back, framed by brown sheets, with the sun coming in through the skylights above, Luke looked so good her heart swelled in her chest. "I want to be with you when you tell Jess about us."

"All right. Maybe that's a good idea, since he needs to know we were involved in New York. Come over around one." She cocked her head. "You didn't have plans today, did you?"

"Nope." In a sudden move, he hiked himself up, grabbed her shoulders and kissed her hard. "I'm all yours, sweetheart."

I hope so. She didn't say the words aloud, but she meant them in her heart. Last night had been wonderful and special, and she felt such a connection to Luke it frightened her. But she quelled the doubts. Time to think positively.

Once she arrived at the house on Fifth Street, Jayne found a note on the counter saying Eleanor was at a church meeting. Jayne had called the older woman the night before to say she wouldn't be home. Poor Eleanor probably thought she was with Ben. Jayne didn't correct the assumption because she wanted to keep her relationship with Luke to themselves for a while, except for Jess, and especially around the site. A private person by nature, she didn't want to have to deal with what other people thought of them as a couple. Luke hadn't been happy about that but had reluctantly agreed.

Hurriedly, Jayne showered. After changing into a yellow cotton sundress, she was sipping strong black coffee in Luke's gazebo, going through a stack of magazines, when Jess appeared on the porch of the house. He called out, "Hi, Jaynie. Let me get some coffee. I'll be right there."

As she waited for Jess, she watched the birds chirp and skitter at the feeder, basking in the warm early summer morning, just like Jayne was doing. Jess came back outside, took the porch stairs at a clip and covered the distance to the gazebo with a spring in his step. He dropped down on one of the benches across from her. Up close, framed by Luke's loving gift to Eleanor, Jess's shoulders were more relaxed and his face less lined with stress than they had been when he left.

"You look better," she said. "More at peace."

"I am. The time away was good for me. I figured some things out."

"I'm so glad. Tell me."

Cupping the mug in his hands, Jess stared at a nest that a bird was building in the rafters. Finally, he said, "I lost sight of certain things these past few weeks. I love Naomi, and I'm going to work on our relationship until we get it right. I'm moving home today, if she'll have me."

"I think that's best."

He faced her fully. "I'm not abandoning you, Jaynie. I'll be here for you, too. There's got to be a way to work this out if we all try hard enough."

Giving him an encouraging smile, she said, "You just worry about yourself and your family. I'm okay."

He studied her face. "You look better, too."

"I am."

"Why?"

"Finish what you were saying first."

"I'm embarrassed about what I did to Luke. He's my best friend, and I attacked him. What's more, I had no right to say what I did about him. Don't get me wrong, he isn't above doing whatever he has to in order to get his way, but if he was using you, he did it with a good heart."

"He wasn't using me, Jess."

"I sincerely hope not. In any case, I'll apologize to him right away. The rift between us over you has to end."

"I'm sure that will make him feel better." She glanced at her watch. "He's coming here about one."

"That surprises me."

Oh, just wait. "I have to talk to you about something else."

"What?"

From behind Jess, she saw Ben walk into the backyard, where she'd told him to meet her. Today, he dressed in casual slacks, Dockers and a golf shirt, but his expression was anything but relaxed. Obviously, Ben was nervous.

Before Jess noticed him, Jayne said simply, "Jessie, Ben Scarborough's in town. We talked last night, and he's here to see you."

"What? Ben's in town?"

"Actually, he's standing behind you."

His head whipped around and Jess saw the person who had been almost as good a friend to him as Luke and Timmy. The two men stared at each other, neither moving, not saying a word.

Please let this be a good idea, Jayne whispered in silent prayer.

AT TWELVE-THIRTY—hell, he couldn't wait any longer—Luke drove over to Miss Ellie's. He didn't go around front and ring the doorbell; he'd seen a fancy rental car and Jess's Jeep in the driveway, so he figured the big pow wow between Jess and Scarborough was going on. He'd guessed they'd be in the house and he planned to wait in the back, where he found Jayne alone in the gazebo.

Since she didn't notice him, he took a minute to study her: she looked so pretty in her yellow outfit, leafing through a magazine. Bright rays snuck in below the roof, bathing her in sunlight. For a minute, he was overcome by what he felt for her; something had happened between them last night besides the sex—something, as he'd told her, that hadn't happened with any woman but her. And Luke welcomed it, embraced it, rejoiced in it.

When he neared the structure, she looked up. And he saw in her eyes and in the intimate smile she gave him that she felt the same way he did. That knowledge only enhanced his feelings. "Hi, love," he said meaningfully.

"Hi, there."

When he reached her, he tipped her chin and kissed her, tasting her sweetness. "Everything okay?"

"Jess is back. Ben's inside with him."

"I figured." He dropped down next to her. "How'd Jess react when he saw Scarborough?"

"He was stunned. I don't know how he'll feel about what Ben has to say. They went inside right away."

Picking up her hand, he smoothed it with his thumb. Her skin was always velvet soft. Feminine. And she smelled great. "Was the retreat good for him?"

"Yes. He's going back to Naomi."

"That's great news."

"It is. Combined with Ben's apology, Jess will be happier, Luke, I know it."

"Even when he finds out about us?"

"I think we can manage that one."

Bringing her hand to his mouth, he kissed it, then

laced their fingers. "I want it to be good between us this time, Jayne. To stay good."

She put her head on his shoulder in a tender gesture that made his heart stutter. "I want that, too."

Thank the good Lord. Luke had no time to wallow in their declarations, though, because Jess exited the house alone, let the back door slam and headed for them. When he reached the gazebo and saw them together as they were—close, with hands linked—he shook his head. "This is a surprise. Jeez, they're popping up all over the place this morning."

"It's a good one, Jess," Jayne whispered. "I promise."

When Jess remained silent, Luke added, "Me, too, buddy. I promise it is."

ROSA CORELLI WAS a solidly built woman with salt-and-pepper hair and a nice smile, if and when it graced her face. She'd given birth to five children who resembled her with their dark hair and eyes, but every one of them was taller. Wearing simple tan pants and a pink blouse, Rosa sat across from Jayne at Sunday dinner, the scent of spicy marinara sauce and pasta filling their lovely home.

It was obvious that Rosa also held sway with each and every one of her offspring—including Luke. He was seated next to Jayne, his dad next to him. His sisters and their respective husbands lined the rest of the table—Belle's spouse Nick and Teresa's Jonathan, but not Cal Sorvino. The kids were outside, eating the hot dogs their grandpa had roasted for them.

Rosa took a bead on her son. "We all went to St. Mary's this morning, Luciano. Except you."

Luke nudged Jayne with his leg. At the time, she

knew, he'd been in bed with her. She hoped her face didn't color, but she stared down at her plate just in case. It was filled with mounds of spaghetti and meatballs, and she'd been trying to put a dent in it.

"Sorry, Mama. Maybe next time."

His father, the elder Luciano, was a solid, working-class glassblower, now retired. He squeezed his wife's hand where it rested on the table. "Not in front of his girl, Rosa."

His girl. Jayne warmed to the term. But when she glanced up, she couldn't help but notice that Luke's sisters exchanged arched eyebrows and frowns and one of them cleared her throat. In truth, Jayne had been scared spitless about coming to the Corelli Sunday dinner, and it was as hard as she'd thought it would be when they'd arrived just in time to eat. But when Luke had asked her to accompany him, in that soft, coaxing way of his, she'd been helpless to deny him. For a moment, she'd panicked about the power he held over her. It had only been a week since Ben had come to town, a week since she and Luke had made love again and reawakened old feelings that she believed she was ready to accept now.

"Jayne," Belle said calmly. She was closest to Luke and also Naomi, but she'd been the kindest today. "Does your family attend church?"

"Yes." She told them where. Rosa didn't look happy about the Methodist part.

"God says the way to heaven has many paths," Luciano pronounced and stood. "Now, I think dinner is over. Very good sauce, Rosa, *mi amore.* Nick, Johnny, Luke, let's go to the backyard and check on my grandchildren. We can take a look at my tomato plants while we're there."

Luke shot a worried glance at Jayne, which heightened her unease. "I'll help the girls clean up," he said.

"Since when?" Corky, the oldest, stood too. "You go out and keep an eye on the kids. Mama, you come into the kitchen and sit." Corky seemed to fall into the oldest sibling role easily, making Jayne wish she had sisters.

Standing, Luke reached for Jayne's hand. "Jayne can come with me."

"No," the girls said at once.

Corky added, "The five of us will clean up."

Luke gave Jayne a puppy-dog look and followed the other men out.

Swallowing back her discomfort, Jayne rose and picked up plates. With all of them helping, they cleared the table quickly. The kitchen was big but homey, with two stoves, an oversize refrigerator and a huge table in the center, where Rosa did indeed take a seat. Corky crossed to the sink, where a triple window overlooked the backyard, ran water and began to rinse dishes. She was heavier than the others but had the best hair: a shiny dark brown with natural curl. She'd seemed preoccupied all during the meal, though, and when she glanced outside, appeared wistful. Again, Jayne wondered why Cal hadn't come to dinner. She hoped nothing was wrong, but she'd found Cal to be up and down in his moods.

Teresa, the next oldest, petite, pretty and sporting an almost black braid down her back, began to scrape the dishes and hand them to her sister. Maria, the businesswoman, divorced, stored the food and efficiently ordered Belle, the prettiest, to make espresso and put cookies on the table.

She also handed Jayne a towel. "You dry."

They went about their business in utter silence, during which Jayne caught all of them giving her not-so-surreptitious glances. She kept her head down or her gaze averted, and prayed this awkward ordeal would soon be over. She was going to kill Luke for leaving her alone to face his sisters, no matter that he'd tried to prevent it.

When they finished cleaning up, Rosa sniffed. "She did okay. She didn't buckle under pressure."

Corky wiped her hands on a towel and turned to face Jayne. "She's tougher than she looks."

Teresa chuckled and addressed Jayne. "The others have run out on us to join the guys when we gave them the silent treatment."

Relief pumped through Jayne. "You do this to all Luke's girlfriends?"

"He hasn't brought that many home," Belle told her gently. She crossed to the table. "Come sit. We won't bite your head off."

"Well, that's a relief." Jayne was totally unbalanced by these formidable women in Luke's life but was trying not to show it. Seated with the five of them around the table, sipping the espresso Teresa had served, she waited to see what they would say to her.

"I'll start." This from Belle. "Luke's a wonderful man, Jayne, but he has a controlling streak." She rolled her eyes. "He thinks he can fix everything."

"I know. It's been directed at me more than once."

Again, Teresa jumped in. "He's got the biggest heart of anybody I know, but he's stubborn."

"Yep, I agree." Jayne shrugged. "I can handle that."

Maria took her turn. "He's great with our kids, but needs a family of his own."

Biting her lip, Jayne squelched a giggle. "If you're going to ask my intentions, I *am* going to bolt."

Rosa smiled, then grew serious. "My boy's complicated. And he's never gotten over Timmy dying."

"He blames himself," Jayne said. "He told me all about it."

Corky set her cup down, her expression puzzled. "He never talks to anybody about Timmy. Not even us."

That surprised Jayne.

She decided to clear the air. "Okay, look, I care about Luke. Very much. And I think he cares about me. I know he's a good man, and I want to see where this goes between us. But I'm not making any promises. For what it's worth, neither is he."

As if everyone needed time to digest that, Rosa stood, went to the cupboard and brought back a tin of cookies. When she opened it, the sweet smell of chocolate—from the round little balls covered with frosting—wafted over to Jayne. Everyone took one and nibbled.

Belle began the conversation again. "Fair enough, Jayne."

"So you're going to give me a chance?"

Teresa snorted. "It wouldn't matter if we didn't. He has a mind of his own."

"Oh, no, you're wrong. It would matter a great deal. One thing I know about Luke is how much he loves all of you and counts on you."

Maria cocked her head. "You buttering us up?"

"No, but I would if it would help you accept me."

Again, they laughed, the feminine chorus filling the air.

"Consider us buttered," Corky told her.

Then Maria leaned over and squeezed her arm. "Be careful with him, Jayne. He's been hurt too much already."

By her, too, which was apparently something his family didn't know, so she didn't tell them.

"And don't coddle him." Corky again.

"But spoil him a bit." Teresa shrugged a shoulder. "He's used to that."

"I want you to love my boy like we do." When Jayne showed surprise at his mother's use of the word *love,* Rosa held up her hand. "We know him. We know how he feels just seeing you two together."

"For what it's worth," Belle added, "we can tell how you feel about him, too. By the way you are with him."

Jayne was at a loss for words. Wisely, she again kept quiet. She'd save her comments for Luke himself. One thing was for sure. She was going to follow Teresa's advice. After him leaving her alone to deal with the Corelli women en masse, she wasn't going to coddle him tonight.

FROWNING, Luke pulled up to the site next to Jayne's Lexus five minutes after she'd arrived. As he got out of his truck, clouds drifted overhead. That wasn't what was bothering him, though. This was so stupid, her refusing to drive to work with him after staying the night at his house—the past ten nights, to be exact. For some stupid reason, she was hoping to keep their relationship a secret from his crew. He'd even resorted to sending her sexy e-mails and text messages when they weren't together, which had been fun but still secretive. She'd finally told Miss Ellie about the two of them because Jayne had been away most nights and didn't want the older woman to worry.

He wanted to shout their new bond from the rooftop of the house. Yet he'd succumbed to Jayne's demand. How could he not? She held far too much sway over him, and he was powerless to stop his headlong vault into their relationship.

He caught sight of her over by the tree on the side of the lot with Cal, examining the blueprints spread out before them on a couple of sawhorses. A variety of things had to be recalculated because of the changes Jayne had made in the floor plan. She'd agreed to work with Cal on any needed revisions in the wiring to accommodate the new laundry room. Because Harmony Housing was building twenty-five units in all, the changes had meant they'd had to reorder materials. For some reason, his brother-in-law hadn't been happy to get Jayne's input, but Luke never could figure out Cal. He looked okay now, though, and was smiling at her.

"If you're going to keep this thing between you two a secret, you'd better stop watching her like you're a football player who has the hots for the head cheer-leader." Jess spoke from beside him, his tone teasing.

"I know." Luke ran a hand through his hair. "Hell, I wish she didn't want to hide what's between us."

"She's a private person in a lot of ways."

That concept was foreign to Luke, given the family he came from. He turned to Jess. A week ago his friend had accepted Ben Scarborough's apology *and* Luke and Jayne's relationship with quiet equanimity and wished them well. Though Jess had been pissed off that they'd kept their past relationship from him, he'd eventually forgiven them that deceit, too. Then he'd gone home to work on his marriage.

"How's it going with Naomi?" Luke asked as they headed for the trailer.

"It's better now that I've moved back into the house. I hate that we're walking on eggshells around each other, but it is what it is." He sighed. "At least last night we finally…" He trailed off as if he realized he was thinking aloud.

"Slept together?"

"I didn't say that." Jess was private in some ways, too, which Luke used to tease him about mercilessly.

"You didn't have to. I can tell."

Jess nodded to Jayne. "She okay?"

"Couldn't be better."

Luke's gaze rested on Jayne as she stood and stretched. The graceful bend of her back made him think about the steamy night they'd spent together.

But he scowled as Mick O'Malley approached her. And, shit, what was he doing? He said something to her. She nodded and he circled around to put his hands on her shoulders. Began to massage them. It was a way-too-intimate thing to do, and Luke started toward them.

Jess held him back. "Leave it. Interfering will only make things worse. He always went after the girls you liked."

"Think he knows?"

"Yeah. He always did. Come on inside, I want to schedule the first inspections."

"Okay. She's moved away from him, anyway."

They juggled things for an hour, then Luke left the trailer to check on the progress inside the house. He loved this part of the building process, when the innards of the structure were installed. In a way, the wiring and the plumbing were like the systems of the body, giving life to the building itself. He caught a glimpse of Jayne hauling plywood with the reverend and walked over.

"Jess needs you in the trailer, Jayne," he lied. "I'll finish this with Pastor Wilkins."

"Oh, okay, thanks." She gave him a cute smile and left.

But she wasn't smiling when she stormed back a few minutes later. "What do you think you're doing?"

"Helping with the plywood," he said innocently.

"Jess didn't want to see me." God, he loved it when she was full of fire like this.

"Sure he did."

"No, he didn't." Her eyes narrowed. Reaching out, she grabbed his arm, said, "Excuse us, Reverend," and dragged Luke out of the house and around the corner, where they could be alone.

"You did that on purpose," she hissed softly, so no one would hear them. "You didn't want me lifting that wood."

He threw back his head, tipped his hard hat and hitched his hip cockily. "So, sue me."

Jayne fumed and laughter bubbled out of him. He couldn't help it. She was such an easy mark sometimes, and it didn't take much to rile her.

"Don't you dare laugh at this, Luke Corelli. I still haven't forgiven you for leaving me alone with your sisters yesterday."

"Why? You passed the test."

She was so mad she sputtered. He glanced around and when he saw that no one was watching them, he grabbed her waist and kissed her hard on the mouth. She tasted of anger and her own personal sweetness. "Gotta go. We'll settle this later at home. In bed."

As he walked away, she regained her powers of

speech and swore at him until he got to the trailer and could no longer hear her curses.

"WHAT DO YOU DO, cast a spell on me?" Jayne was lying with her head on Luke's bare chest, drowsy from their vigorous lovemaking.

"If I do, you cast one on me, too." He kissed her hair. "That was mind numbing."

"Hmm."

They cuddled close for a minute. Then Luke added, "I wanted to ask you something."

She tensed. "Is it bad?"

She always expected the worst, a habit he hoped to cure her of by proving he wasn't like the other men in her life, including her father.

"No. It's not bad." He ran a hand down her bare back as he spoke. "On Sunday, Maria asked if we'd watch Analise this weekend. Then she'd return the favor and let us have her cottage on Keuka Lake for a long weekend. Jess owes me a few days off."

Jayne stilled. "We?"

"Yes. Stay here for the weekend. Help me take care of the kid. Then we can have a whole four days at the lake with no interruptions."

That sounded heavenly. "Okay. It shouldn't be too hard to babysit one little girl, especially with that kind of motivation."

"Ha! You don't know her. She's a demon child."

"Who's totally enamored of her Uncle Luke."

"What can I say?" Laughter rumbled in his chest. "Now that's settled, want to go another round?"

He flipped her on her back. "You just want me for the sex, sweetheart?"

He looked so handsome with his hair tousled, his face relaxed and teasing. This Luke was devastating.

"Must be because I was mad as hell at you at the site today."

"I got that." He lowered his head and kissed her chest.

"I'd prefer no one at work find out about us."

"I know." He pulled the sheet down.

"But you don't care?" she asked, a trace of concern in her voice.

That stopped him. He looked up and straight into her eyes. "Of course I care what you think. It's just that I want everybody to know we're together. I can't understand why you don't."

"I…what if it doesn't work out between us?"

His whole body stiffened. "Oh, that's just what I wanted to hear."

"Maybe we should be taking things slower."

"Too late for that, Jaynie."

"Is it?"

Now he stilled completely. "It is on my part."

When she didn't answer right away, he started to draw back.

"No, wait. Luke…" She tugged him over her again. "I guess it is on my part, too."

He smiled. "Now that didn't kill you, did it?"

"No, actually, it felt good to say it aloud."

"Then it'll feel good to tell everybody."

"You just don't know when to stop, do you?"

The devil came into his eyes. "Nope," he said and ducked his head under the covers.

Minutes later, she was begging him *not* to stop.

CHAPTER ELEVEN

"'AND THEN, Nancy Drew looked at her father. He frowned and said…'"

"'If you really want to go, I'll take you.'" Analise finished the paragraph before Jayne could and smiled with the cocky self-confidence of her uncle. Luke's niece had been second guessing the next lines of the story for the past half hour.

The little girl was insatiable in demanding both Jayne's and Luke's time this weekend, but she was so damn cute, with her light blond hair and blue eyes, that neither adult had been able to refuse her much. Poor Maria, when she came home to this spoiled child. Even Krystle, their dog, had gotten the royal treatment, and snoozed now at the end of one of Luke's spare beds. Jayne couldn't believe how much she enjoyed taking care of both the girl and the puppy.

"Where's Uncle Luke?" Analise asked when the chapter ended and Jayne set the book aside.

"He's over at your house, fixing your bathroom faucet."

In addition to asking them to watch the child and the dog, Maria had left a list of chores for Luke to do at her house, a block away from his home. Now that Jayne had gotten to know his sisters, she took pleasure in watching them boss Luke around.

"I love Uncle Luke."

So do I.

Oh, Lord, where had that come from? Was that how Jayne really felt? Her first impulse was to deny it. She didn't want to be in love with Luke yet. Things were just getting back on track for them. And, in some part of her heart, Jayne was still afraid that every man she came to care about would turn on her. On the other hand, she'd vowed to be optimistic about their relationship.

"Time for bed, honey."

Analise shook her head vehemently, sending her wispy hair flying. Her mouth formed a perfect pout. "Not till Uncle Luke gets back."

"I suppose we could wait. What do you want to do until then?"

"A makeover."

"You're too young for a makeover."

"Am not!" Now the girl scowled just like her uncle. "We got the stuff over there." She pointed to a vanity that Luke had built in this room.

Jayne had been awed when she discovered what Luke had done to the second floor of his house. He'd remodeled his bedroom, equipping it with skylights, a warm wood ceiling and a lot of masculine accents. He'd also torn down the wall between it and the second bedroom, making a desk and computer area.

But what surprised her the most was the way he'd remodeled the rest of the upstairs. He'd created two kids' rooms, one for the nieces who came to visit and one for the nephews, each with furniture and decor befitting their gender. Hence, the vanity.

"Don't you think those things are for the older girls?"

Jayne asked of the makeup and hairstyling accoutre-
ments on the vanity.

"I'm not a baby."

Resigned, Jayne slid off the bed, pulled Analise up by
the hand and crossed to the vanity. Krystle woke up,
trotted behind them and sat at their feet, watching
intently.

Jayne was in the process of curling the girl's hair
when Analise said, "You're nicer than any of Uncle
Luke's other girlfriends."

"Thanks for the compliment."

"How come?"

"How come what?"

"How come you're nicer? Do you like him better
than they did?"

Jayne laughed out loud. "You know what? Maybe I
do."

LUKE FOUND Analise and Jayne in the girls' bedroom.
Scents of perfume and hair spray filled the air. From the
doorway, he watched Jayne put something on her own
eyes. He had thought Analise would run her in circles,
but she seemed okay.

"You know, both of you are too pretty for that war
paint."

Analise peered over at him. Oh, man, Maria was
going to kill him. The kid looked about sixteen. His eyes
dropped to the floor and he saw they'd even put a pink
bow in Krystle's hair. But then Jayne turned, capturing
Luke's full attention. She never wore much makeup—
just something on her lips and maybe her cheeks, so
he'd never seen her *done up,* not even in New York. He
couldn't believe it. She was runway-model gorgeous.

The stuff on her eyes accented their violet color and her cheeks shone with something iridescent.

"Close your mouth, Uncle Luke," she said, smiling.

"I…I…holy cow, I'm dazzled."

"Don't get used to it. I can't be bothered with all this on a daily basis."

"You don't need it."

"What about me, Uncle Luke?"

He focused on Analise. "Who are you, missy? I came looking for my niece."

Analise giggled and blushed. "It's me, Uncle Luke."

"Nah." He walked closer. "You're a young lady. I want my little girl back."

Grinning hugely, Analise threw herself at Luke. He held her close and over the child's head, he saw Jayne watching them. Suddenly he was hit with the same thoughts he'd had during their picnic, the day he sat in the ants—thoughts about pregnancy and children and marriage. This time, he freely admitted his notions were linked to the beauty before him.

SOMETHING WAS WRONG with Luke today. They'd driven up to Maria's cottage on Keuka Lake joking, teasing and trading sexy innuendos about having four whole days together and what they'd do with their time. Luke's explicitness had made her warm, as had the way he'd run his hand over her bare knee. When they'd arrived, they'd moved their things into the cottage quickly so they could take the boat out.

Now they were on the water, with the June sun beaming down on them, the air warm enough for shorts and tanks, but Luke's mood had turned dark. It had changed right after he'd gone into the kitchen to get the keys to the cabin cruiser. Jayne found him staring at Maria's refrigerator, the sadness on his face bone-deep. When she'd asked what was wrong, he'd said in a clipped tone, "Nothing."

Since then, he'd only spoken to her to help her with the boat. Jayne tried not to read anything into his mood. Just because he was normally upbeat when they were together didn't mean he'd always be happy. He was entitled to bad moods. Hadn't she seen a lot of those before they'd become a couple again?

But why today, when he'd been looking forward to this holiday together so much? Had he brought someone else up here? Was he having second thoughts about how quickly this relationship had developed?

He has a rep with the ladies...

I never liked how he treated the women he dated...

You're nicer than Uncle Luke's other girlfriends...

No! Jayne was not going to do this! Luke had gone a long way toward restoring her faith in herself as a woman, and she'd be damned if she'd backtrack now. She wouldn't let her insecurities get the better of her. Standing, she approached him where he stood at the wheel and slid her arms around his waist. He was hot and sweaty, but she laid her face against his back anyway. He started, as if he were somewhere else. As if he'd forgotten about her.

"I need to know something," she said softly.

"What?"

"Can we stop the boat for a while so we can talk?"

"There's this little cove I want to show you." His tone was gruff. "We'll stop there."

So, she waited, reseated on the front bench, watching the sun bounce off Luke's head and the wind ruffle his dark hair as he steered, anchored, and finally took a seat next to her.

"I'm sorry," he said, surprising her.

"Don't be sorry. Tell me what's wrong."

He stared out at the water, softly cresting from the wake of another boat that sped by. "I saw Maria's calendar."

"What was on it?"

"She…they all must…she had today marked."

"Today?"

"I…it's the anniversary of Timmy's death."

Jayne reached for his hand. "Oh, Luke."

He squeezed her fingers tightly, making them ache. "I forgot. Hell, I *forgot* this year."

"It's all right that you did."

"No," he barked. "It's not. I can't ever forget. If I'd remembered, I wouldn't have come up here with you."

Don't take offense. Give him what he needs now. This isn't about you. These were murky waters for her but, damn it, she was determined to navigate them well.

"What would you have done instead?" she asked gently.

"Gone off on my own like I always do." He shook his head. "I wonder if Maria remembered and set us up to come here on purpose. The girls hate it when I disappear."

"I'd hate it, too."

"Don't do that, Jayne!" He let go of her hand. "It's my right to grieve."

"I thought we were both working on the mistakes we'd made."

"I am. But to forget the day he died, not to mourn him, no way."

Jayne was quiet for a good long while. Then she stood. "Let's go back to the cottage. I'll pack my things and take the car back to Riverdale. You can grieve all you need to this weekend, and I'll come and get you Monday night."

His eyes widened, the lines still deep around them. "You'd do that for me?"

"Of course I would." She nodded to the wheel. "Come on, let's go."

When they reached the shore, she helped him dock the boat, preceded him into the cottage and went upstairs to pack. When she finished, she found him on the porch, beer in hand, staring out at the crystalline lake. Feeling so sad she could barely breathe, she approached him from the side.

"I'm sorry this anniversary is hard for you, Luke. I wish you'd let me help, but I respect your right to handle today the way you want." Kissing his head, she turned and started away.

He grabbed her arm. "Don't go."

Oh, thank God.

Before he could change his mind, she circled around the chair and knelt down in front of him. She wasn't shocked to see his face wet, because she'd seen him cry over Timmy once before. Jayne felt like crying herself.

"I don't want to do this the old way." His voice was so gravelly she could hardly bear it.

"That's good, Luke."

He searched her face. "I don't know what to do, though."

"What would Timmy want you to do?"

Tears fell down his rugged, masculine cheeks. He leaned his head back against the chair and closed his eyes. Then the corners of his mouth turned up. "He'd tell me to quit being such a pussy. That he was dead, it wasn't my fault, and I needed to go on with my life. He'd bitch me out and tell me not to lick my wounds anymore." Luke opened his eyes. A soft smile. "If he saw you there, on your knees, he'd tell me to take advantage of you."

She arched a brow. And reached for his belt. He stayed her hands. "No, come here first." He dragged her up so she straddled him. He cradled her head against his shoulder. "Stay here, like this, for a minute."

"Whatever you want."

Luke held her close and stroked her back as waves lapped on the shore and the sun began to set. Jayne was content to stay there with him. Finally, he roused himself.

She drew back. "Ready?" she asked, smiling.

"For what?"

"To take advantage of me? Like Timmy would want."

"Yeah, I'm ready."

Jayne rejoiced in the fact that Luke was willing to let her comfort him today. It felt better than any gift she'd ever been given.

LUKE AND JAYNE STROLLED along the streets of Penn Yan, heading for the outdoor market that set up every Saturday at the town park. The day was glorious, with birds singing and the sun shining so hot that Jayne had put on a sundress and straw hat. Luke couldn't believe how good he felt today, given the memories that always plagued him this time of year. And it was because of the woman who walked beside him, her arm linked with his.

He was falling in love with her. It didn't scare him, though. He felt truly happy for the first time since he'd left New York.

"What are we buying?" Jayne asked as they reached the market. Dozens of vendors lined the perimeter of the park, canopies overhead, tables spilling out tomatoes, strawberries and whatever else the townspeople fancied.

"Picnic food. I'm taking you to the cove for a summer supper."

"Sounds good to me."

"Hmm." Everything sounded good to him today.

They wandered through the stalls, picked out fresh Wisconsin cheese, crusty bread from a local bakery and succulent strawberries. Luke made a mental note to stop at the liquor store to get wine, maybe even champagne. When Jayne veered off down a smaller aisle, Luke paid for the food and followed her.

She was kneeling in front of a makeshift stand where a little boy and his father were selling…what? Puppies? Luke grinned at the four tiny pups nipping at Jayne, letting out cute little squeaks and soft barks.

"My dad says we can't keep them," the towheaded boy was telling Jayne. "So I gotta find a home for them."

Luke joined Jayne on his knees and knuckled one of the dogs. "Are they purebreds?"

"Uh-huh. Full Yorkies." Just like Krystle.

"You could get more money than what you're asking for them."

The father smiled. "I know, but we're going to live overseas for a year and can't bring dogs. We just want a good home for them and were hoping for some takers today."

Luke hadn't noticed the puppy nearest the boy.

Jayne saw her at the same time. "Oh, look, Luke, she's got a hat on."

"Yeah, it's from one of my sister's dolls." The boy rolled his eyes. "She calls her Hattie."

The father frowned. "We need someone to take them before the kids get too attached."

"Aren't you a sweetheart?" Jayne whispered as she picked up Hattie and cuddled her close.

"Like her?" the boy asked hopefully.

Jayne gave the puppy one last nuzzle, then put her down. "I do." Standing, she added, "But I'm in no position to have a dog."

"Aw…" This from the boy when the pup arched toward Jayne. "She already likes you."

Luke took Jayne's hand. "Sorry."

Jayne sighed. "Me, too."

They walked away. When Jayne was silent, he asked, "You want the dog?"

"No, I can't." She slid her arm around his waist. "I'll have to settle for you."

He chuckled. "Well, hell, I don't think I've ever been compared to a mutt before."

"Yeah, but you're such a cute one."

They'd almost reached his car when Luke handed her the keys. "Go ahead and get in, turn on the air. I gotta hit the Porta Potti back there."

"Hurry, though, we don't want to lose too much of the day."

"We won't."

He took longer than he'd planned, but they made it to the cove by six for their picnic, and it was fun. After the emotional connection they'd made Thursday night, there was an ease, a comfort, between them that had deepened and become more significant.

"What are you thinking?" she asked, from across the bow.

"How great this weekend is going."

"I know." She sipped the wine he'd bought.

He checked his watch, then gave her a cocky grin and nodded to the cabin. "Wanna go down below with me, darlin'?"

"Why Mr. Corelli," she said, batting her eyelashes, "are you suggesting something salacious out here on the water?"

He wiggled his eyebrows "Yep."

She stood abruptly. "Fine by me."

They had some damned hot sex before they headed back. He was at the wheel, whistling, when from behind him, Jayne asked, "Why do you keep doing that?"

"Doing what?"

"Checking the time."

"Am I?"

"You have been for the last hour."

"I, um, don't want to get caught in the dark on the lake."

They arrived at the shore before the sun went down. Luke docked the boat and, once they were inside the cottage, he said casually, "Why don't you shower first?"

She slid her arms around his waist, smelling of fresh air and sunshine. "Why don't we shower together?"

"Not tonight. I want to catch the news on TV."

Again, she looked skeptical. "Are you sure nothing's going on?"

"Not a thing," he lied.

Luke heard the bathroom door close upstairs just as

there was a soft knock at the front of the cottage. *Perfect timing,* he thought as he headed to the foyer.

JAYNE SLIPPED into a white tank top and blue pajama bottoms and, towel drying her hair, wondered what had gotten into Luke tonight. He wasn't in a bad mood, but he'd been acting strangely for the past hour. She'd forgotten there were so many facets to him and wondered happily how long it would take her to discover all of them.

Smiling at the thought, she descended the stairs into the living room. All the windows were open, letting in a warm breeze off the lake. Luke was in a far corner. He'd showered, too, probably in the tiny stall off the kitchen. His hair was still wet, he wore cargo shorts and a T-shirt, and he was slouched in a chair, grinning.

"All right," she said. "What's going on?"

He pointed to something. On a small table against one wall were a bottle of champagne and glasses. And from below came tiny yips. Dear Lord, there was a dog crate there.

"Oh, Luke, oh, dear, what did you do?"

"Go see."

Rushing across the room, she dropped to the floor and unlatched the crate. Out hurtled the puppy in the straw hat from the market. "Hattie, hello, baby." She cradled the tiny animal to her chest. The puppy had soft as velvet hair, fragile little bones and big somber eyes.

Hattie licked Jayne's face, making her giggle. For a few precious seconds, Jayne took pleasure in the puppy's antics then, still on her knees, looked up at Luke. "I can't keep her, Luke, you know that. I couldn't impose a dog on Eleanor, and even after I leave Riverdale, my life isn't set up for a pet."

He looked startled, then he frowned.

"What?"

"I hate to hear you say things about going back to your old life." He scowled. "You said you wouldn't run again."

"I won't, but neither of us knows how our relationship will turn out."

"I don't want you to even *consider* leaving Riverdale."

"Luke, I—"

"Move in with me, Jayne."

Jayne almost dropped the puppy. *"What?"*

Rising, he came toward her and poured the champagne. He drew her up, took the dog, placed the puppy in the crate again, then handed Jayne a glass. "Live with me, sweetheart. Let's give what we have together a real shot."

It only took Jayne a moment to decide, "Yes!"

LUKE WAS on top of the world as he and Jayne drove up to the Harmony Housing Tuesday morning. They'd stayed at the lake last night, where they'd cemented what he'd hoped was an unbreakable bond, and slept together with the comfort of that knowledge wrapped around them like a blanket. She'd moved into his house this morning, which was why they were late getting to the site—it was already ten o'clock. And since Jayne was no longer determined to keep their relationship a secret, he kissed her soundly before she slid out of the car.

She said only, "Bad boy," and took off toward the volunteers.

The site was unusually quiet, Luke noticed as he

fished his hard hat, work gloves and tool belt from the truck bed. When he circled to the front, a man approached him—Mark Johnson, the electrical inspector for the units.

"Hey, Mark," Luke said cheerfully. "I forgot you were coming today."

"Yeah, I was here at seven." He held up a set of blueprints. "We got a problem, Luke."

"With what?"

"The wiring in the house. Take a look." Mark spread the plans on the truck's hood. "See these sections I marked off?"

"Uh-huh."

"The wiring's the wrong gauge in them."

"The wrong gauge?"

"Yeah. You used fourteen instead of twelve like in the rest of the house." For some reason, in wiring designation, the higher the number, the lesser the quality of the gauge. "What's more, there's no ten gauge in the laundry room."

"That's impossible." Wet spaces needed better grade wiring with thicker cables.

"I can see from the prints that these were the areas in the house where changes were made from the original blueprints."

Luke thought a minute. "Yeah, we had another architect consult on this. She wanted layouts changed and found a way to put in a laundry room and do some other things at minimum cost."

"Well, the changes were cheaper in part because of the thinner wiring."

"Wiring doesn't cost that much…" He trailed off when the facts gelled.

"I see you understand. Multiply the savings by the twenty-five houses you're ordering for and better wiring adds up. Plus, the price of copper's skyrocketed since Hurricane Katrina, so there's added savings."

"It's still not a ton of money."

"It would be thousands. Maybe she thought that was significant savings."

"Jayne doesn't have anything to do with costs for the project. Jess Harper takes care of all that."

"Then maybe she just made a mistake."

A mistake? Luke thought. Jayne made *another* mistake?

CHAPTER TWELVE

JAYNE LOOKED UP when Ed Ranaletti came into the house. Its frame was finished, the plumbing and electricity were in and they were planning to install the insulation today. Then the drywall would go up. But for some reason, the crews hadn't started yet this morning. Instead, when she'd arrived, she'd found a group of them waiting inside the structure.

Ed stood in front of the assembled workers, paid as well as volunteer, and announced, "We aren't gonna be doing the insulation today."

"Why?" Jayne asked.

"Don't know." He tipped back his hard hat. "Luke called a halt just before he and Jess took off in Jess's Jeep."

"Luke left the site?" Jayne wondered where he and Jess would have gone so suddenly, and why Luke wouldn't have spoken to her first. She was still feeling the warm, dreamy effects of this morning…

He'd carried her bags inside his house and set them down in the foyer, then turned her to face him. "I want you to consider this your home, now. Our home. We both feel the same about buildings, structures, and this one is yours, too." He'd reached over to the table by the door. "Here's a key."

"Oh, Luke." She'd thrown her arms around him, pushing aside those small, nagging concerns that this was all happening too fast.

A very male chuckle. "Happy?"

"Very much." Then she'd kissed him. They'd barely made it to the bedroom.

As he made love to her—in *their* bed, he'd called it—he whispered, "I'm falling in love with you, Jayne."

He hadn't stopped touching her until they parted at the site.

Wondering where he was now, she hoped nothing was wrong.

"What are we going to do today?" one of the other volunteers asked.

Before Jayne heard the answer, her phone rang. Maybe it was Luke. She fished the thing out of her pocket and clicked on. "Jayne Logan."

"Jayne, this is Carrie." Her firm's assistant.

For a moment Jayne's whole other life came crashing back—Logan Architects in California, the mistake she'd made with the Coulter Gallery, her career possibly ruined. She was shocked to discover she'd been so caught up with Luke in the past few days that she'd nearly forgotten about her professional circumstances. Her staff had returned to work this week and she hadn't even called the office.

Carrie said, "I have some bad news."

Jayne began to shiver, despite the heat of the day. Telling Carrie to wait until she could speak privately, Jayne walked out of the house and around to the side. "What is it?"

"Two more of the 2011 projects have been canceled. I contacted the other clients we've got on board before

I called you, and they were evasive. They said they'd wait for the final decision by the architectural board, but they didn't sound enthusiastic about using us."

So, her career was over? Just like that? Jayne was stunned.

But again, she thought of Luke—his comforting words, his assurances that she'd get through whatever happened. And he'd be there with her every step of the way.

Okay, then, she could handle this.

"Jayne, what should we do here?" her assistant asked. "I'm not sure why you haven't come back to L.A."

The two other architects had a few loose ends to tie up, but they'd been waiting for the preliminary drawings she was supposed to have done and instructions from Jayne on the contracts Logan Architects still held.

She dropped down on a stack of plywood, and its familiar scent comforted her. She remembered how she'd always loved the smell of newly cut wood on one of her sites, and her throat clogged. Would she lose all that?

"Jayne, are you there?"

"Yes." She had to take care of business. "Set up a conference call for later this afternoon with John, Marissa, Tom, you and me." She glanced at her watch, then at the house. No work to do today, really. "Call me when you have a time everyone's available, and we'll discuss this."

Forcing herself to stay calm, Jayne clicked off and stared at the trees at the back of the lot. If her career was over, what would happen to the people who depended on her? She needed to talk this through with Luke. He'd help her decide on immediate action. So she punched in his cell phone number. She'd feel better if she could even hear his voice.

When he didn't answer, she was puzzled. That puzzlement became tinged with panic when she realized how much she was depending on him right now. How she'd promised herself she'd never depend on a man like she had relied on Ben.

But damn it, she was done thinking that way. Luke wasn't Ben, and this wasn't the time for second thoughts. She could trust Luke, she knew she could. And the rest of her life would work out.

JESS AND LUKE SAT across from each other in the Family Diner with the Harmony Housing plans spread before them. The scent of strong coffee permeated the room. Luke usually liked the way it smelled, but the mug at his elbow turned his stomach.

"I can't believe it," Jess said. "How could she make this kind of mistake? It's a no-brainer."

"Which is why I'm not sure she did."

Luke sounded more confident than he was. *Someone* had made the mistake, all right. But it didn't have to be Jayne. Maybe it was Cal. When he found himself wishing his brother-in-law, a member of his own family, was the guilty one, Luke was ashamed of himself. But God, it couldn't be Jayne. The consequences were untenable.

"What other explanation is there?"

"Maybe Cal knows something."

Luke's phone buzzed. He hoped it was his brother-in-law. Luke had called him earlier, but he hadn't answered. Both Cal and Mick were missing from work this morning. Neither had phoned in.

He checked his caller ID. "It's Jayne."

"What are you going to say to her?"

"I don't know. I'm not picking up right now."

When the phone stopped buzzing, he looked up from it. He knew his own expression was grim. "She'll be despondent if she's made another mistake, Jess. I'm not sure either one of us can help her with that. Her professional confidence is already at an all-time low."

Jess shook his head. "Maybe we could keep this from her."

"How?"

"Make up a story. Don't tell her about the problem and fix it when she's not there." He raked a hand through his hair. "Hell, I don't know."

Luke glanced away from Jess and scanned the diner. The lunch crowd hadn't come in yet, so there were few people here. Thinking about Jess's suggestion, Luke idly noted a man on the other side of the divider, and another one seat over. He stared blindly at the backs of their heads. "No. I'm not going to lie to her."

"It was a bad idea anyway."

"Damn it. Things were going so well between us."

"That doesn't have to change."

"Our relationship is precarious, Jess. She's still skittish about trusting me. Seeing Scarborough didn't help."

"I can't believe he offered her a job."

"He wants *her* back."

"Yeah, that was pretty clear."

Jess's easy acknowledgment made Luke's fist curl around his mug. "Over my dead body."

"Easy, boy. We'll figure this out."

Just then, Luke's phone buzzed again. He grabbed it, checked the caller and clicked on. "Hey, Cal, where have you been? I've been trying to reach you."

"I'm sick." His voice was hoarse.

"Sorry to hear that. Why didn't you phone in?"

"I overslept. I was just about to call when I got your message."

Luke rolled his eyes at Jess and mouthed, *Sick.* Then into the phone, he said, "Cal, we've got a problem with the wiring. I need to talk to you about it."

A very long pause.

"Cal?"

"I been throwing up. And got diarrhea. I can't leave the house."

"All right, then, listen carefully." Luke had wanted to do this in person, but the phone conversation would have to suffice. "Do you remember when you met with Jayne on the wiring for the altered plans?"

"Just a minute…I gotta go."

Luke waited. "Cal's really sick," he said to Jess. "And heading to the bathroom, as we speak."

It was an interminable length of time before Cal came back to the phone. "Sorry. You wanna know about the house wiring?"

"Yes, on the altered plans for the changes Jayne suggested."

"Ms. Hotshot Architect made the decisions on that. I just followed her instructions."

"Are you sure?"

"Yeah." Luke heard the sound of a cigarette being lit Cal couldn't be that sick. "Why?"

"The inspector came today and said the wiring's the wrong gauge in the changes."

"Hell. I told her she was going too high on the wiring. She wouldn't listen. Got all offended that I'd question her expertise. She's a bitch to work with, Luke. I don't like her any more than you do."

Cal hadn't been at Sunday dinner with his wife when Luke brought Jayne to meet his family, but surely Corky would have told Cal that Jayne and Luke were together. Luke didn't want to get into any of that now, though.

"Are you positive Jayne insisted on the higher gauge wiring for the changed parts?"

"Yeah. She said it would save thousands of dollars. I think she wanted credit for saving the team money."

As Luke had told the inspector, that didn't make sense. There weren't any problems with their budget.

"Cal, why didn't you come to me with this? Particularly about not using ten gauge in the laundry room."

"The laundry room?"

"Yeah. We've got fourteen gauge in there, too."

"I didn't know about that."

"The cables are all different colors. You'd have to know."

"Oh, that's right. Zeke Huff wired that area. He didn't tell me anything was wrong, though."

Something didn't fit, but Luke couldn't put his finger on it.

"What's going on?" Cal asked hesitantly.

"I don't know yet. I'll be in touch."

When Luke disconnected, Jess was shaking his head. By the time Luke finished telling him everything, his friend was scowling. For a moment, only the low murmur of the waitresses and the door opening and closing filled the space between them.

Then Luke said, "I can't believe it." He racked his brain for some plausible explanation, or even a clue. "Did we save thousands on the wiring?"

"No paperwork came through. It's probably too soon to get the bill. I do think Johnson was right about that.

If these changes were made, we could save money, especially when the price of copper's gone up."

"Jayne wouldn't concern herself with that. She must have been wrong, is all." Luke swallowed hard. He kept coming back to the same thing. "Jess, why is she making all these mistakes suddenly in her career? Even with simple things like laundry room wiring."

"You son of a bitch."

Startled, Luke looked up into the enraged face of Mick O'Malley. "Mick? What are you doing here?"

"I was sitting over there." A bit drunk from the look and smell of him, which was probably why he wasn't avoiding his bosses. "I heard you blaming Jayne for some problem at the site. You're a bastard, Corelli. You don't have a loyal bone in your body."

"Now wait just a second."

Mick swore again and walked away.

Rattled, Luke sat back and closed his eyes. "Just what I need."

"Forget about him. We have to come up with a plan for talking to Jayne."

Luke drew in a heavy breath. "We'll present the problem to her, give her Cal's story, and let her tell us hers."

"I don't see what else we can do."

"Just hope there's a logical explanation for what she did." Luke took out his phone. "Meanwhile, I have to make some calls to redo the wiring."

"Ripping out the used cables and rewiring the areas will cost a bundle."

"I'll pay for it."

"Luke…"

"No, Jess, I will, but that's not important now. Taking care of Jayne is."

It was a testament to Jess's concern that he didn't argue, as he always did, about Luke using his own money on the site.

JAYNE WAS SITTING behind the desk in the trailer, wondering why Luke hadn't called her back, when the door opened. She smiled over at the entrance, but it wasn't Luke who stood there. It was Mick O'Malley.

"Hi, Mick. I thought you were off today."

"I am." He looked terrible—unshaven, his clothes wrinkled enough to have slept in.

"I came over to talk to you. I heard something you need to know about."

"Shoot. Things are pretty much suspended on the insulation. Nobody knows why."

Crossing the room, Mick stood before the desk. He looked even worse up close. "I do."

"Yeah?"

"The wiring in the new sections is the wrong gauge."

"The wrong gauge?"

"Yep, higher than the original specs called for."

She shook her head. "That's impossible. Cal Sorvino and I worked on the rewiring together. Luke asked me to consult. I know everything was up to code."

His face sad, Mick dropped down into a chair in front of her. "Jayne, Luke and Jess were meeting downtown at a diner just now to discuss the problem. They got Cal Sorvino on the phone and I overheard them. Cal says it's your fault, that you recommended a higher gauge, and they believed him."

"You must be mistaken. Luke wouldn't believe something like that—at least, not without talking to me first."

"I'm sorry. I swear to God I heard him ask Jess why you were making all these mistakes."

All these mistakes? Had she screwed up again?

Mick added, "Corelli can't be trusted, Jayne."

Jayne just stared at Mick, her mind blank, her body frozen. For a minute, she felt nothing. Then fear started to seep in.

Like a robot, she listened to Mick offer more details. She responded. He left. All the while, the ghost of inadequacy immobilized her.

But when he was gone, she came out of her daze and, in her mind, went over the meetings she'd had with Cal on the changes she'd recommended. Rising, she crossed to the file cabinets and withdrew the office set of plans and the new orders, sat back down at the desk and examined the revised sections of the blueprints. And there it was. Gauge fourteen for everything. Even the laundry room.

But Jayne knew, *remembered,* she'd recommended the same wiring in the new parts as was in the rest of the house, and for the laundry room, she'd gone with ten gauge, which was the best wiring for wet areas. She and Cal hadn't even discussed altering any of it.

So why was Luke doubting *her?* Did he really think she was incompetent and would keep making mistakes?

No, she wasn't going to believe that. Not until she talked to him, told him what really happened. After hearing her take on it, he'd come to a different conclusion, if indeed Mick's assumptions were correct. Who was to say Mick hadn't misunderstood a conversation he was eavesdropping on?

Jayne sighed heavily. Everything would be all right. There was some kind of mistake. She hadn't done anything wrong this time. And Luke would believe her. She knew he would.

DREADING THE CONFRONTATION with Jayne, Luke entered the trailer with Jess. Head bent, she was sitting at the desk, making notes, and glanced up when he came in. His heart broke at the relieved expression on her face. "I'm so glad you're back. Both of you."

"We had some business to discuss."

She frowned. "Yeah, I know."

Jess asked, "What do you mean?"

Jayne stood, circled the desk, hitched a hip onto the edge and folded her arms across her chest. She seemed a bit stiff, but other than that, Luke couldn't read her mood.

Before she could speak, Luke crossed to her and ran his knuckles down her face. "Sweetheart, we found an error in the wiring for the new sections of the house. The ones that you consulted on with Cal."

"I know."

Oh, God, it was true, then? She *knew* she'd made a mistake?. "The inspector found the error."

"I know." She picked up the plans. "These show the same thing."

Dear Lord, could this be more incriminating? He and Jess exchanged looks. They'd need to alter their tactics now that she'd admitted she'd made a mistake.

Jess sighed heavily as he walked over to the desk. "This is all going to be okay, honey."

She cocked her head. Her violet eyes were wide and confused. "What do you mean?"

Feeling oddly guilty, Luke explained, "We talked to Cal this morning. He said you told him we didn't need the gauge we'd used on the rest of the house and that we could go with the higher one to save money."

"I did no such thing." Her brow furrowed when both of them continued to stare at her.

"You just said you knew about this," Jess put in softly.

Staring at the man she loved, Jayne hesitated to accuse Mick because she didn't want him to get in trouble for coming to her.

"Baby, it's all right. It'll be hard to accept that you made another mistake. But I'll pay to fix it, and Jess and I will keep the problem to ourselves."

"You think you can *fix* this? By covering up a mistake?" She shook her head. "Of course you do. You think you can fix everything."

"No, I mean, yeah, I will fix it. But it'll be okay."

"I didn't change the wiring gauge."

"You just said you know about the error."

She shifted, feeling uncomfortable and increasingly angry. Luke shouldn't need to know Mick's role to believe her. "Um…somebody told me about the problems."

He stared at her. Jayne realized what he was thinking.

She watched him, a pit forming in her stomach. "You believe Cal and not me?"

"He said he didn't do anything wrong."

Her jaw dropped. "You believe Cal, even though I'm telling you I didn't make a mistake, either, and that directly contradicts his story?"

"Cal wouldn't lie."

"But I would?"

"No, I didn't mean it that way."

"Yes, Luke, you did." She faced Jess. "You think I made a mistake, too?"

"It's okay, Jaynie."

Jayne shook her head at the accusations made by the two men she cared about more than anyone else in the world. The two men standing there in broad daylight, calling her a liar. The two men who believed she'd made another error, who probably believed she'd *keep* making errors, because they thought she was incompetent. She didn't know which hurt more: that Luke thought so little of her after what they shared, or that neither he nor Jess believed her when she told them the truth.

She slid off the desk. "All those assurances, Luke? That my reputation could withstand one mistake. That everybody makes them. That I was an excellent architect. They were all lies?" She cursed the crack in her voice.

Even as both men protested, "No, sweetheart," and "No, Jaynie," she cut them off.

"I can't believe I thought I could trust you two." She felt her eyes mist. "This is just like college, Jess, where we were falsely blamed." She took a bead on Luke. This was the hardest, and she felt sick inside. "And you, you're just like Ben." Another man she had loved, turning on her. "I can't believe it."

She started to circle around them because she was crying. Both men blocked her way.

"Jayne, we've got to talk about this," Jess said.

"Jayne, baby, listen to us—"

"Listen to what?" She swiped impatiently at her cheeks. "You've already made up your minds." Again, she started out.

Luke grabbed her arm. "I'm not letting you leave like this."

"You can't stop me, Luke. Not that it matters, but for

the record, Mick came here and told me he overheard you and Jess. That's how I knew a mistake had been made."

"Jayne…"

"None of that matters," she said. "Not after you chose your family over me."

"I'm not letting you go until we've hashed this out."

Before Jayne could say anything more, Ed Ranaletti burst into the trailer.

"Luke, something's happened."

"Not now, Ranaletti."

He held up his phone. "Yeah, now. Your sister's trying to reach you. You haven't picked up, so she called me. There's been a car accident involving your brother-in-law. It's bad, Luke."

AT THE KITCHEN TABLE, Jayne willed away the remnants of the blinding headache she'd gotten on her way over to Eleanor's house. She finished off a letter to the older woman, who was out shopping, thankfully, so Jayne didn't have to say goodbye to her in person. Ruthlessly trying to keep her emotions at bay, she set the missive next to the copy of the plans she'd made when she and Cal had figured out the new wiring schematic. Her habit of always duplicating work whenever she designed or changed something, brought on by her college problems, had paid off. Because, clearly visible in her drawing, and her notes, was the designation of twelve-gauge wiring for the rewired parts of the house—the gauge used in the original plans. And the laundry room sketch indicated ten-gauge wiring. She had *proof,* not only her word, which Luke didn't believe anyway. She also put a personal check for ten thousand dollars next to the letter—the amount of money it would take to fix a mistake that someone else had made.

Jayne scanned the kitchen, which held a hint of the scent of Eleanor's Earl Grey. She'd always loved this homey room. But she was done here in this house. Done in Riverdale. Completely and utterly done. Somewhere in her heart, she'd known it had been a mistake to come to town, and she'd been right.

When thoughts of Luke intruded—where he was, who had been hurt in the accident and how bad it was— she banished them. She wouldn't feel sorry for him. Or guilty for walking out on him when this terrible thing had happened. She refused to let herself think about that.

Standing, she made her way into the foyer and left the house by the front so she wouldn't have to look at the gardens, either. There was only so much loss she could take today, and she still had a major hurdle ahead of her.

She drove like an automaton to Luke's house. Its imposing presence had warmed her only this morning, wrapped itself around her like a parent, and Jayne had felt as if she'd been accepted by a loving family. Steeling herself against the loss, she got out of the car and used the key he'd given her a few hours ago to let herself in.

She became immobilized in the entry. The space smelled like Luke, and it nearly cracked her reserve. But she'd already broken down once, something she'd vowed never to do again after Ben's betrayal. She wouldn't repeat the experience. Keeping her eyes straight ahead, blocking out the little yips coming from the kitchen where they'd settled the puppy this morning, she climbed the stairs to the bedroom. Unable to help herself, she crossed to the bed and her composure slipped. Sitting down, she picked up Luke's pillow and brought it to her face. Again, his scent encompassed her and she remembered his words…

I'm falling in love with you…

You can trust me, sweetheart, I promise…

I'll always be here for you, Jayne. I promise, you aren't alone anymore.

The last broken vow hurt the most. She'd felt alone for most of her life—with the exception of Jess and Eleanor for those few years—and the belief that she wasn't anymore because of Luke's promise had been a lifeline. But at the first test of his loyalty, he hadn't stood by her. He'd categorically sided with someone else.

Tossing the pillow aside, she rose, got her bags out of the closet and packed her things. Since she didn't have much to gather up, she was out of his room in a half hour. She stopped in the bathroom to get her toiletries and caught sight of the shower, where she and Luke had made love. She sniffed the trace of aftershave, stared at the razor he'd left on the sink. Those small details made tears threaten again, so she thrust her things in a case, hurried out of the room and fled down the steps.

The puppy yipped soulfully, and Jayne started toward the kitchen. Maybe she could take Hattie with her.

But no. That would be impossible. The dog would remind her of Luke every single day, and Jayne couldn't bear that. Instead, she set the key on the foyer table and, with the woeful cries of the tiny dog in her head, she left Luke's house and sought the refuge of her car.

Inside, she realized she had no idea where she'd go. It didn't matter much anymore, she guessed. Just so she was away from Riverdale, away from Luke Corelli and the hope he'd engendered in her.

Once again, she'd been foolish to believe in happily-ever-after.

She was on the outskirts of town when she realized she was running away again.

You're good at running, he'd said to her.

Well, about that, Luke had been right.

CHAPTER THIRTEEN

LUKE HELD a sobbing Corky in his arms as his other sisters gathered around them. The ringing of phones, the constant din of the intercom, and the smell that all hospitals couldn't escape filled the air. But Luke was tuned into Corky's grief and fear. "I...I can't believe it, Luciano. I can't."

He held her tight, as much for himself as for her. "Wait until we hear what Nick has to say, Cork. Wait until you get an official report from Cal's doctors." Even to his own ears, Luke's tone sounded unconvincing, so he hoped Belle's husband could get some news for them soon. Nick was a neurosurgeon at Riverdale Hospital, and though he wouldn't be working on a relative's case, he'd gone right into the emergency room when Cal had been brought in.

Corky said, "You don't understand. It's bad. It's really bad."

Belle hunched down in front of them. "Let's see what Cal's doctors tell Nick, honey." Despite her words, when she looked up at Luke, Belle's expression was bereft.

Luke tugged Corky closer. "It'll be all right."

Belle shook her head.

Oh, dear Lord, Cal wasn't going to make it?

A few minutes later, their mother and father burst in through the door to the waiting area. They'd been out shopping when Cal had spun into a guardrail while taking a curve too fast. In the middle of the freaking morning!

They hurried to Corky and Luke. Rosa said, "*Bambina,* come to your mother." She drew Corky up so both parents could hug her.

Luke rose, pulled Belle to the side, and gave her a hug. "Do you know any details?"

"He was drunk."

"At this time of day?"

"Apparently he tied one on last night and his alcohol content was still high this morning. Hell, he could have been drinking all night, for all I know."

"I just talked to him an hour ago."

"About what?"

When the circumstances surrounding Jayne entered Luke's mind, he mercilessly squelched his thoughts. "It's not important now." Nothing was, but Cal's survival. Especially not a coldhearted bitch who could walk away from him after he'd gotten such devastating news. No, he wouldn't think about Jayne Logan for a good long time.

Belle nodded to her older sister. "It's bad timing for them, if there ever was a good time for something like this."

"What do you mean?"

"They've been having problems, Luke. Corky just told me this morning. Cal had been sleeping in the finished basement for weeks. They were barely speaking."

"Why?"

"His drinking got out of hand. His erratic work schedule, being off weeks at a time, was wearing on them. Corky thinks some other things were going on, but she's not sure what."

"Shit." He scanned the waiting area. His sisters were now comforting Louie, Corky's oldest. Jess had gone straight for the younger Sorvino kids after he'd driven Luke here. Naomi and Miss Ellie had already arrived a few minutes before them. All the people he loved were in this room. Minus one. Again, he wouldn't go there. "Why did Corky keep this to herself, Belle?"

Belle reddened.

"Isabella? Why?"

"Cal didn't want you to know. He was afraid it would affect his job with Harmony Housing. She said they were fighting a lot about money."

That hurt, Corky not confiding in him, but he pushed it aside, too. "She could have told you or the other girls. She must have been going through hell trying to deal with this alone."

Despite the gravity of the situation, Belle snorted. "Since when could we ever keep secrets? She knew we'd tell you."

That, too, made him feel bad. He'd been staunchly supportive of Cal, and his other two brothers-in-law, though he'd never liked Maria's ex. Why did people see him as such an ogre?

His phone rang and, for a moment, Luke froze. Then he said, "I'll take it outside." He found his way to the front of the hospital, thinking the caller might be Jayne, checking to see if he was okay. What would he say if it was? How could she have left him at a time like this?

The call wasn't from Jayne. It was from Ed Ranaletti, asking about Cal. While he had his foreman on the line, Luke put Ed in charge of the project until he returned. Depending on what happened, who knew when he or Jess would be back.

From behind, he heard, "Was it her?"

He turned to Jess. "No, Ranaletti." Luke felt himself weakening. "How could she have left me now, Jess?"

Expecting a defense of Jayne—that she wasn't thinking straight, that she had this thing about trust and he'd betrayed it, or that she was scared—he was chagrined when Jess shook his head.

"I don't know, Luke. She shouldn't have gone, no matter what she was feeling about us at the moment."

He never expected Jess to take his side over Jayne's. It should have made him feel good, but instead, it sliced him to the core.

ONCE INSIDE her father's Manhattan apartment, Jayne found it necessary to lean against the wall for support. Just being here threatened her composure. What had she been thinking to come to the place where she'd lived twelve years ago, when Luke and she were together? They'd made love on the leather couch against the wall, cooked dinner in that kitchen off to the right, and fallen asleep together in the bed in the next room.

But she'd had to come if she was going to pursue the course of action she'd decided on.

She guessed she could have gotten a hotel room until she could rent another apartment, but she'd been pretty much incapable of doing more than calling her firm back and getting herself to the city. Maybe being here would help in the long run. Maybe memories of Luke would make her recall why she'd left him in the first place. She hadn't trusted him then, and he'd proved yesterday that she couldn't trust him now.

That part of her life was over, and she'd start anew here if it killed her.

Turning her mind to business, she thought about the conference call she'd made to her staff at a rest stop. She'd told each of them to look for another job, promising each a hefty severance package. She couldn't keep them hanging any longer.

With a despondent sigh over her shattered professional circumstances, she headed to the bedroom but veered off to the spare—damn, she couldn't go to the main one—climbed under the covers fully dressed and took a two-hour nap. When she woke up, though, she was immobilized. All she could see was the tortured expression on Luke's face when he'd said, *You can't be serious. You're going to leave now?*

Without answering, she'd walked out the door. Coldly and cruelly. She'd run again, at a time when he really needed her. And in the stillness of her father's guest room, Jayne admitted it had been a horrible, horrible thing to do. But all she'd wanted was to flee the pain, and in doing so she'd let down the man she loved when he was at his lowest.

Of course, his refusal to believe her had been wrong, too. But, here in the dark, her own actions couldn't be rationalized and, once again, Jayne felt bad about the person she'd become.

To quell the self-recriminations, she reached over to the nightstand and picked up the phone. She kept repeating words in her head as she waited for the connection. But they weren't Luke's words. They were Ben's.

I own my own outfit. It's big and successful…I want

*you to come to New York…we'll find something for you
to do. You can have your pick of projects to consult on.*

And she would, damn it. She'd do it, if for no other
reason than she had nothing else in her life.

IN THE WAITING ROOM of the hospital, Luke sprawled on
a vinyl-covered two-seater, his feet up on a low table.
Corky was asleep on a long couch and the other girls
dozed in chairs. His parents had stayed the night too.

Nick, Belle's husband, came out of the emergency
room. Easing up, Luke crossed to him.

"How is he?"

Nick shook his head. "Not good." Nick was one of
the best neurologists in his field, making the import of
his words grave. "He's still in a coma. If he'd come out
of it, we'd have more hope."

Cal had undergone surgery at about ten last night to
have his spleen removed. It had been irreparably
damaged in the accident, and he also had a broken leg
and some nasty bruises. He was in pretty bad shape.

"Damn it."

"How's Corky doing?"

"She's taking it hard. Seems like she and Cal were
fighting, big-time. They have problems, more than we
knew."

"Marriage is tough," Nick said, glancing at his own
wife.

Luke remembered Belle talking about her frustration
with Nick when he and his sister had played racquetball. "You and Belle okay, Nicky?"

Nick shook his head. "Fighting about stupid things.
It's times like these when you realize how petty your
gripes are."

Luke only wished that were true about his trouble with Jayne. Off and on, he'd thought of her all night. He wondered where she was, *how* she was. Around three this morning, he admitted to himself how much his believing Cal over her must have hurt, especially given her history with men, especially after the promises he'd made to her. Had nothing else happened, they might have worked the whole thing all out. In light of what he'd discovered about Cal in the past several hours and what she'd told him about Mick, Luke admitted he might have been wrong about the wiring problem. But regardless of that, the fact that Jayne had coldly walked out on him, knowing how important his family was, *not* knowing who was hurt or how badly, had done irreparable damage to their relationship. She'd run, just like she had before.

"Luke, you okay?" Nick asked.

"Yeah, sure. I just hope Cal is."

"Me, too." Again Nick glanced over at the family. "Let's go see them. Belle's waking up."

With a heavy, heavy heart, Luke watched Nick cross to his wife. She smiled up at him, and Luke bet a lot passed between them in the looks they gave each other. Couples fought, made up and lived their lives together.

Not him and Jayne, though. Not after she'd abandoned him when Cal's life hung in the balance.

BEN SAT across from Jayne in his office on Lexington Avenue, with the city a backdrop in the glass wall behind him. His firm took up a whole floor and the office was as impressive as hers in Los Angeles. Right now the place buzzed with ringing phones, humming computers and people conferring on different projects. Jayne had missed those sounds of business.

"Do you have any idea how thrilled I was to get your call this morning?" Ben asked, smiling.

"I've changed my mind."

"So you said. What happened to the guy in Riverdale?"

Jayne had been honest with Ben that night they'd had dinner at the Baron Steuben. She'd told him she was going to be dating Luke to see where that relationship took them. Little did she know it would go nowhere.

"It didn't work out."

Ben steepled his hands. "I wish I could say I was sorry."

"It was stupid to…" Oh, God, she felt her eyes mist again.

"Do you think you might change your mind about us personally?"

"Oh, no, Ben. I can't even think about something like that now."

"All right."

"Do you still think there's something I can do here at your firm?"

He smiled reassuringly, and she remembered believing in that smile. A lot like she'd believed in Luke's. "Of course. Have you any idea when the decision about your license will come down?"

"I called my lawyer this morning. No word yet, but he promised to check with the board this week."

"If you get it back, we're home free. You can simply sign on as an architect." He leaned over his desk. "Even if you don't, I promise we'll find you something that utilizes your talent." He straightened. "Again, I'm so glad you came to me."

I had nowhere else to go.

Against her will, Jayne remembered saying the same

thing to Luke. He'd told her about his sisters and how they'd brought him back from an emotional blackout after Timmy died. Suddenly, she wondered who'd been hurt. How badly. How the Corelli family was holding up.

No, she wouldn't go there. She'd concentrate on getting a job and pulling her professional life together. Once again it was all she had, and she'd been foolish to think otherwise.

"Come down to the drafting room. Let's take a look at the projects we have going and where you might fit in."

When he stood, she said, "Wait a second, Ben. Are you sure you trust my judgment? After what I've done with the Coulter Gallery?"

"Yes. I know better than anybody about costly mistakes and second chances." He circled his desk and waited for her. "I trust you and your judgment. I only hope, someday, I can earn back *your* trust personally."

Jayne wondered if she'd ever trust a man again. Thinking not, she stood and let Ben grasp her elbow and lead her out.

CAL WAS TRANSFERRED to the Critical Care Unit and Luke and his family waited for three days for him to wake up. They'd gone home to change and shower, take care of kids and pets, but all the adults had returned here and slept on couches or cots. Unable to face his house, Luke had asked Naomi and the girls to take the dog—permanently, he hoped—and he'd cleaned up at his parents' home.

On the third day, when their moods were so somber Luke felt as if the whole room might combust, Nick came out of CCU smiling. "Cal's awake. He's confused, and sore as hell, but he's going to make it."

Corky dissolved. Her kids had left with Teresa's

husband to sleep for a few hours, so Corky could break down at Nick's pronouncement. Luke took her into his arms and hugged her.

When she finally quieted, Nick asked, "Want to go see him?"

"Uh-huh." A hiccup. "I do."

Luke stayed Nick's arm as Corky walked ahead of him. His brother-in-law's face was pale with fatigue, but held relief now, too. "Does he remember anything?"

Nick shook his head. "He's disoriented, which is common after head trauma. He keeps mumbling 'I'm sorry, I should have told you.' When he saw me, he said, "'Luke, I should have told you.'"

"He thought you were me?"

"Brother-in-law thing, probably. Do you know what he was talking about?"

"Yeah, something at work that he should have reported to me but didn't. Can I go in?"

"Later today. Just his wife and kids for a while."

Luke blew out a heavy breath. "I should check in at work. Maybe I'll head over there now."

After bidding goodbye to his family, Luke left the hospital. The drive to the site made him realize how exhausted he was. He couldn't even think straight and decided to touch base with his guys and then go home and crash. Sooner or later, he'd have to face his own place and the memories of Jayne that lived there.

He found Jess in the trailer. "Your mother called me. I'm glad about Cal."

"Yeah, me too. How are things here?"

Jess shook his head. "We redid the wiring and the insulation's in."

"I saw the drywall going up." Reaching into his back

pocket, he drew out his wallet. "I got the check for the wiring stuff."

"That makes two of you."

Dropping into a chair across from Jess, Luke scrubbed a hand across his face. "What do you mean?"

"Jayne left ten thousand dollars to cover ripping out old wiring and installing new."

That surprised him. And hurt, for some stupid reason. "So, she admitted she made a mistake?"

"No, she left these, too." Jess held up what Luke recognized as plans for the units. "With a letter for my mother."

Luke wouldn't feel bad she didn't leave word for him. Damn her, how could she just abandon him? "What are the plans for?"

"Since college, Jayne has been religious about duplicating her work. She apparently made copies of the changes she and Cal made."

"What does that matter now, Jess?"

"These show the recommended ten-gauge wiring for the laundry area and twelve for the rest. It's all right here."

"We saw fourteen gauge on the original set."

"Which means someone's lying. I'm not so sure who, now."

Remembering Nick's comments about Cal's muttering, Luke shook his head. "It's Jayne."

"Are you sure?"

"When he woke up, Cal kept mumbling, 'I should have told you.' Men coming around after a coma don't lie, Jess. He felt bad for not telling me about the wiring."

"Cal could have meant something else." Jess rapped

his knuckles on the set of plans Jayne had left. "How do you explain these?"

"I don't have to."

Jess shook his head. "When we confronted her, she said she knew about the problem because of Mick. Not because she made the mistake."

"So what if she talked to Mick? That doesn't mean she didn't make the error in the first place." Abruptly, Luke stood. "I'm not even going to consider that she wasn't lying." He pointed to Jayne's check. "That's blood money if I ever saw it. And you know what, keep it for the wiring. She can pay for her own goddamned mistake."

"Isn't that a bit cruel?"

Luke recalled Jess saying that to him when Jayne first came to town and he'd tried to run her off. It seemed like a lifetime ago.

Furious, he rounded on his friend and felt his control slip. "Cruel? I'll tell you what cruel is. She abandoned me when the news came about Cal. Damn her, she knows how I feel about my family and she just left me alone to deal with it."

"Because you believed Cal and not her."

"Whom you doubt now and I don't. I was wrong about Jayne. Very, very wrong." He started out.

"Luke?"

"What?"

"If Cal was in such bad shape about Corky and other things, maybe he lied to us."

"He didn't. My family wouldn't lie to me about anything. We're not that way, and apparently Jayne didn't understand that."

"You're a mess, buddy. Almost as bad as when

Timmy died." At Luke's angry look, Jess held up his hand. "No, let me finish. You couldn't do anything about losing Timmy, but you can fix this with Jayne."

Luke pounded his fist on the doorjamb hard enough to send sharp pain up his arm. "No! And listen to this, Jess. Listen good. If you and I are gonna stay friends, we won't ever talk about Jayne Logan again."

CHAPTER FOURTEEN

THE MUSCLES in Luke's lower back screamed as he picked up a case of shingles from the bed of his truck and hoisted them onto a dolly. The roofers had come up short and he'd been the one to fetch more. He was pissed about it, like he was pissed about everything these days.

Not that it mattered what he did. Nothing seemed to have meaning, not even seeing the current Harmony Housing don its outer shell. Usually, he rejoiced in the finishing touches of a project—the windows, the roofing, the siding. Now, a week after Cal's accident, he took no pleasure in his work. Even the heavens reflected his mood. Dark clouds threatened overhead, and he hoped to hell they got the roof finished before a downpour.

A vehicle pulled into the parking lot just as he'd loaded the last of the shingles. Luke was surprised to see Belle's van. Exiting the front seat, she watched him walk toward her. "What do you want?" he asked.

"Good morning to you, too."

He tore off his work gloves and stuffed them in his pocket. "Sorry. But all of you have been hovering. Even Dad."

His sister plopped her hands on her hips and, despite

the fact that she looked like a wisp of a thing in a white sleeveless top and shorts, she seemed formidable. "Because *you've* been such a bear. You missed Sunday dinner yesterday."

"I wasn't hungry."

"You look like shit."

"Thanks, my ego needs stroking." He turned back to the truck. "Go away."

"Cal's come home from the hospital and wants to see you."

That stopped him. He pivoted to face Belle. "Cal refused visitors all week. Corky says he's depressed."

"They've been talking a lot."

"Why me?"

Belle shrugged a shoulder. "I don't know. Guess you'll have to find out."

"I'll call him."

"No, Corky said just to go over there as soon as you could."

"Goodbye, Belle," he said, giving her his back for a second time to walk away.

"Have you heard from Jayne?"

He halted and looked up at the gloomy sky. God, he couldn't even think about Jayne, let alone talk about her. He couldn't think about Cal because, when he did, it brought back everything that had happened with Jayne. Once he allowed any thought of her in, she plagued him, and the last thing he needed was to replay the events that had caused her to leave Riverdale. The only worse thing to think about was their time together. How she felt, how she smelled, how she came apart when he touched her. "I'm not discussing this."

"Coward."

"Go away," he repeated.

"So you had a fight? Fix it."

You think you can fix this? Like you fix everything else?

He rounded on his sister. "I'm done fixing things. Tell the girls I'm not going to do that anymore."

"Like hell."

"I will *not* talk about Jayne."

"Even Naomi feels bad."

Again, Belle's unexpected news got a reaction. "Why? She did everything she could to get Jayne out of town."

"She's had second thoughts. Even before Cal's accident, she and Jess started some marriage counseling. I think she's getting to a different place about Jess and Jayne."

"Don't tell me Jess is going to see Jayne. Or that Jayne's coming back to town." He heard the panic in his voice. Hell, he couldn't face the dog he'd bought for her, who was still with the Harpers. He'd never survive contact with the woman herself.

"I don't know if she's coming back." Belle opened her car door. "Go see Cal."

He didn't. Instead, Luke kept up backbreaking work all day long. He also continued to bark at anyone who got in his way, alienating those of his crew who were still speaking to him after a week of his rotten behavior.

And he didn't give a rat's ass. He came in at dawn and worked till dark all week. He was just unlocking his truck to leave that night when another vehicle pulled into the parking lot. His father's SUV. The passenger door opened. "Get in," his dad said.

"Dad, I—"

"Get in, boy."

Like many grown men, Luke still couldn't disobey his parents. He slid inside and slammed the door.

Wordlessly, his father pulled out of the lot and drove down the streets of Riverdale. Luke was only mildly surprised to see them drive up to Corky's house.

"Dad…"

His father grasped his arm. "When you didn't go see Cal like Corrine asked you to, she called me. I know what Cal wants to say to you. You have to hear this. Go in, son, and listen."

What could Cal want? Resigned, Luke decided he might as well get this over with. He climbed out of the car along with his father. "I'll wait with Corrine in the kitchen," his father said.

They entered Corky's house without knocking. The ranch was big and roomy, with high ceilings and lots of windows. Corky was off to the left in the family room, sitting next to a hospital bed that had been set up. A low hum came from the TV and Luke could smell the scent of pizza in the air. His sister rose and came toward him; she looked worn-out and…defeated.

Luke's protective instincts went on red alert. "Honey, you okay?"

She shook her head. "Just go talk to Cal."

While his dad accompanied her to the kitchen, Luke crossed to Cal. Man, the guy looked terrible, bruises on his neck and arms, his leg in a cast, and utter weariness etching his whole face.

"Hey, buddy. How you doing?"

"Not good, Luke."

"You'll be feeling better soon. Once the healing starts, it'll go fast. Remember when I broke my—"

"It's not that. Sit."

Why was everybody ordering him around as if he were a child? He took the chair Corky had vacated.

"I gotta say something. And don't interrupt like you usually do. Just let me get it out."

Luke nodded.

"I lied to you about the wiring."

Oh, shit. He hadn't expected this. Or at least hadn't let himself consider it.

"I changed the gauge, then I altered the plans, to get money to pay off gambling debts."

"I didn't know you—" Luke stopped when Cal held up his hand.

"Nobody did." Cal stared at him. "I knew the inspector would catch the mistake, too. I thought I could just blame Jayne and then, when the money went missing, I'd say she needed the cash and pocketed it."

Cal would have no way of knowing Jayne had family trust funds and wouldn't need money.

"There's more. I'm an alcoholic. I can't hold my liquor. Can't even take a beer. Corky's said it for months, but I wouldn't listen. I was still drunk when I crashed the car that morning. I went out because I was upset about lying to you. I should have told you everything on the phone when you asked about the wiring."

Luke remembered Cal saying over and over when he was coming out of the coma, "I should have told you." Luke had misinterpreted what that meant.

And he almost couldn't take it all in. The ramifications of Cal's confession were staggering.

"Let me just say one last thing. I don't expect this will get me off the hook, but I didn't know you were involved with Jayne Logan. I thought you hated her because of what she did to Jess and Naomi. Nobody at work said anything different, and Corky and me weren't talking much, so I didn't know you and Jayne were a couple."

When Luke just stared at him, Cal added, "You can talk now."

"I'm shocked I didn't know what was going on with you."

"Gamblers and alcoholics are very good at keeping secrets."

"Poor Corky."

"I—I know. And the kids, too. They're victims of my weakness."

"Alcoholism is a disease, Cal."

"I guess. As soon as I can move, I'm going to A.A. with Mick."

"Mick?"

"Mick and me, we're both in the same boat. He's going to meetings, too, after what happened to me."

Luke digested that. "Can I do anything to help?"

Cal shook his head. "You're such a nice guy, Luke, it's hard to take sometimes. But yeah, you can watch out for Corky. She doesn't know if she's gonna stay with me through all the legal stuff caused by my accident."

"Always."

Cal laid his head against the pillow. "I'm tired now."

Standing, Luke stared at the man he'd thought he'd known but never did. "Rest. I'll be back." He squeezed Cal's arm and headed out of the room.

So many things whirled around in his head.

Luke had unfairly blamed Jayne.

He had turned on her, like Scarborough, disbelieving her innocence.

But one thing was crystal clear. None of that altered the fact that she had walked out on him at one of the worst points in his life. Even if she forgave his actions, he wasn't sure he could forgive hers.

JAYNE WAS CONSULTING with one of Ben's drafters on a new high rise to go up in lower Manhattan, happy to be back in the thick of the architectural world, when her cell rang.

It was probably Jess again. He'd called her every day and left messages. It had been Cal who was hurt, she discovered when she listened to one, but he'd survived and was recuperating well. There were some things going on she should know about there, Jess said in another message, but he didn't tell her what. He did say that he and Naomi were doing better. The only word on Luke came through the mention that Hattie was living with the Harpers.

Luke didn't even want their dog.

To hell with him.

The phone stopped, and she heard the chime indicating a message had been left. A half hour later, when she was done with the consult, she pulled her phone out of her skirt pocket and checked the caller.

It was her lawyer in California. Her hands shaking, she walked out to the hall and clicked into the message, which said only, "Call me, now."

She'd been in constant touch with Michael and he expected a decision from the architectural board imminently. Was this it? Jayne hurried down the corridor, her heart beating double time. She entered her office, which was bigger and fancier than her position as a consultant warranted, went to the huge window and pressed in the number.

Michael himself answered.

"Michael, it's Jayne."

"You got your license reinstated."

For a moment, she didn't react. She simply froze at the good news she'd wanted badly but didn't dare hope for. Then, for a split second, she wished she could call Luke to share this with him. Chiding herself for the thought, she said, "Th-this is wonderful."

"It is. The board decided you made an understandable mistake. That the bolts could have gone either way—one rod or two. Unfortunately, you picked the wrong one for this particular building."

Actually, the structural engineer had done that, but in the end Jayne had agreed. And she'd been in charge. Her hands were still shaking when she asked, "What does this mean, Michael?"

"As long as your insurance pays the damages to the Coulter Gallery, which it will, you can come back to California and reopen your practice."

"If anyone will hire us."

"There is that." He waited a beat. "You could always stay in New York. You got your original certification there. It might be easier to build up your name away from L.A."

"Well, I don't have to make a decision now. Michael, thanks so much for all you did. I appreciate it."

"Go bask in the good news. I'm sure you needed some."

You have no idea. "I did." Jayne clicked off and rested her forehead against the window. "Thank you, God," she whispered aloud.

"Good news?"

Turning, she saw Ben had come to the doorway. He'd been such a support these past weeks, and she was very grateful. "The best." She told him about her license.

Crossing to her, he picked her up and twirled her in a circle. It was something he'd done when they were young and in love. His big arms banded around her and his scent filled her nostrils.

And neither did anything for her.

"J.J., this is terrific." When he set her down, he hugged her tight. "You can join our firm as an architect now. Do what you love."

"That's a great offer." She drew away and stared into his blue eyes, shining with hope and possibilities. "But it's public knowledge what happened. I'm sure my mistake on the Coulter Gallery is all over the Internet. I may not be an asset to you."

He squeezed her shoulders. "That will take time. But I'll be there every step of the way for you."

Those were the same words Luke had said to her. And, when push came to shove, he'd abandoned her.

"Thanks, Ben. It's an offer I can't refuse."

Not his promise, but the job. Jayne would take the latter, but she doubted she'd ever believe in the loyalty of a man again.

AT EIGHT ONE NIGHT—which promised to be another hellish one—Luke was sitting on the couch in his living room, slugging back a beer and contemplating whether to eat dinner, when the doorbell rang. Damn it, why wouldn't people leave him alone? He didn't want to talk to *anybody*. He wanted to wallow in self-pity, in the permanent lump in his stomach. He heard the key in the lock and looked over to see who was coming to the entrance of the living room. "Miss Ellie?"

She held up the key. "Jess gave me this. I'd like to speak to you, but I understand you're being a hermit these days, or an ogre, depending on who's giving the opinion."

That drew a small smile from him. Clicking the off button on the remote, he stood. "Come on in."

"I knew you wouldn't send me away."

Smart woman. She was about the only person he couldn't kick out, excepting his parents, who'd gone on a short vacation with their closest friends, once they knew Corky was all right.

Taking a seat on the couch, Miss Ellie folded her hands in her lap and smiled up at him.

"Can I get you something?"

She patted the cushion. "Sit." When he dropped down next to her, he noticed the resolve in her blue eyes. "You can go get me Jayne."

He felt himself close down. Every time someone brought Jayne up, he had to force away the memories. Nights were the worst, when his guard was down, or when he dreamed of her, but in his waking hours he did pretty well if people just didn't talk about her.

"She called me," Miss Ellie went on.

That shocked him. "What did she want?"

"To give me good news. And to pass it on to Jess. And to you."

His pulse sped up. "Did she say that? To pass it on to me?"

"Not exactly."

"I thought as much." He expelled a heavy breath. "What happened?"

"She got her architectural license back."

Good for her, he thought. For a minute, pure joy

flowed through him. Then he remembered what she'd done to him, and he deflated like a balloon losing air.

"So she's going back to California?"

"No. She's staying in New York."

That didn't make sense. "Jayne went home? Hard to believe, given how the Logans handled this whole thing."

God, she must have been desperate. After his accusations about the wiring, she'd obviously had nowhere else to go if she'd run to a place where there was absolutely no support.

"She didn't go to the Hamptons. She's staying in that apartment owned by her father's firm in the city."

He remembered the place well. Where it was. What they'd done there. He'd even run across the code to get inside when he'd been cleaning out the basement last week and come across boxes that held records from years ago. "Why'd she go to Manhattan?"

Reaching over, Miss Ellie grasped his hand. Her skin was paper thin and her vulnerability touched him. "She's working in New York." At his blank look, Miss Ellie added, "For Scarborough Associates."

"She went to Ben?" He felt his blood pressure spike. "She went to the man who betrayed her?" Worse than Luke had. "How could she do that?"

"I don't think she had a lot of options, professionally."

What about personally? Damn it all, Luke could still see the guy standing in the sun like some Greek god with his blond hair and blue eyes, begging *J.J.* to talk to him. He remembered again Jess saying Jayne had loved Scarborough, and there hadn't been any man since who meant something to her. She'd gone back to *him?*

Well, screw it. Let her.

"I can see by your face you're putting the pieces together. She'll probably stay with Ben unless you do something."

He shook his head. "No, Miss Ellie. Any relationship between me and Jayne now is out of the question."

"Hmm. Then she's going to be done with you, young man." Miss Ellie stood. "You're both so stubborn."

Luke didn't respond.

The older woman leaned over and kissed his cheek. "Just make sure that's what you want or you could lose the best thing you ever had."

"I already did, Miss Ellie."

The woman's expression was wise. "If you choose to, Luciano. Only if you choose to."

IN THE COOLNESS of an early Saturday morning, Jayne ran in Central Park, trying to shake off the effects of a dream she'd had about Luke. It was another erotic one, and she woke up still feeling his callused fingers gliding over her skin, still feeling him full and heavy inside her. When, *when* would these dreams stop? It was hard enough keeping thoughts of him at bay during the day. Like now, as she weaved around other joggers, Jayne tried to forget the conversations she and Luke had had, but was unable to do so when everything reminded her of him.

I won't jog with you, sweetheart, but I'll rub your back—rub anything, he added, winking, *when you finish.*

She passed by women with cooing babies in strollers…

Do you want kids, Jayne? Because I do.

There were couples, feeding each other doughnuts under a tree…

Hmm, taste this cannoli, sweetheart.

Damn it, would she ever forget him?

When she returned to her apartment, she found another voice mail from Jess on her cell. Feeling lonely and depressed, she let anger at her friend's interference surface. Without listening to his message, she called him back. He answered and she didn't even say hello. "Stop calling me, Jess. I don't want to hear what you think about all this."

He said simply, "Cal lied. We just found out, which is why Mom didn't tell you when you called her."

"W-what happened?"

He explained the bizarre story to her.

Utter shock turned into hope, then fizzled into grim reality. "It doesn't matter, Jess. What's done is done. Luke and I can't go back to where we were."

"Of course you can. Come home and work it out."

"New York is my home now." Though it didn't feel that way yet. But it would. Eventually.

"Are you back with Ben, Jaynie?"

"Not like you mean. I'm joining his firm. But we're just friends."

"Luke's a mess."

"I don't care."

"Look, everybody was wrong in this. I'm sorry I didn't believe you. And you and Luke both let each other down."

"I forgive you."

"Then forgive him."

"No."

After she hung up, Jayne burst into tears. Cal had confessed to lying. That meant this whole thing was all for nothing. Her relationship had been torn apart by

Luke's unequivocal belief in Cal over her and by her leaving Luke when his family was in trouble.

Unfortunately, those were mistakes that couldn't be changed. They'd both have to sleep in the bed they'd made.

What a waste.

CHAPTER FIFTEEN

LUKE HAD PULLED a muscle in his lower back and was so sore he could barely move. His overexertion of the past few days, to banish thoughts of Jayne, had backfired. He had to miss work today, and so his brain was wandering.

No surprise where it went...

First, Miss Ellie's words: *Then she's going to be done with you, young man. Just make sure that's what you want. Or you could lose the best thing you ever had.*

Jess hadn't been any kinder...

You can't do anything about losing Timmy, but you can fix this with Jayne.

Trying to stave off his misgivings, Luke showered and dressed. He was searching for his car keys when the doorbell rang. What now? Ready to blow off steam, he yanked it open.

And his jaw literally dropped.

Mick O'Malley had never been to Luke's house in the six years he'd been back in Riverdale. That in itself was a testament to how much the guy hated him. Now that Mick was here, Luke just stood staring at him. He looked as bad as Cal, minus the bruises and the broken bones; he also seemed even thinner in a ragged T-shirt and ratty jeans.

"Can I talk to you?" Mick asked.

"Yeah, sure." Luke opened the door wider.

Stepping inside, Mick stuck his hands in his pockets and surveyed the interior. "Nice place. I like all the wood."

"Thanks."

Mick nodded to a deck that was visible off the dining room. "Can we go outside? I'm better there."

Where, Luke knew, Mick had often fled his father's fists. Once again Luke felt guilty for not have given Mick the refuge at his home that he'd given Timmy.

On a deck that Luke had built, ironically while trying to deal with the tragedy of Timmy dying, they settled into Adirondack chairs that faced a wooded backyard. Mick was quiet for a long time, watching the trees sway in a cool July breeze. Finally he said, "I was wrong to blame you for Timmy's death."

Luke felt his throat clog. How long had he waited for that absolution? Longer, probably, than even *he* realized.

"Seems like I been mad at you my whole life."

"We left you out, Mick. I understand that now."

Mick faced him. "Yeah, you did. And I hated you for that. But I'm forty-two years old and it's time to leave those things behind." His eyes watery, he added, "And to make amends."

The jargon was familiar. Luke had heard it before. *Mick's going to A.A. too.*

Amends was a big word in Alcoholics Anonymous.

"Okay, Mick. I'm willing to do whatever you want."

"I know it's too late to make up for what I did. Taunting you about Timmy. I hurt so damn much, it was easier to be mad at you than face the reality of my baby brother's death."

"I know something about not facing Timmy's death."

"Can I, um, have something to drink? Nonalcoholic."

"I've got soda."

"That'd be good."

Luke's back pinched mercilessly as he stood. His mind racing, he fetched them sodas. When he returned, he handed a can to Mick and sat back down.

Finally, Mick said, "I feel bad, now, too, because of what I did with Jayne."

"You didn't cause the rift between us, Mick."

"I tried to." He popped the top on the soda and stared down at it. "I knew how she felt about you and I did my best to break you up. I convinced her you'd betrayed her. Now she's gone. I feel like shit because of it."

"Our problems go way beyond what you did."

"I liked her, too." He swallowed. "Not in the way you think. But as a friend."

They sat drinking their sodas until Mick stood. "That's all I got to say, except maybe you can forgive me someday."

"I do forgive you. Right now."

"Thanks." He stared at Luke. "Forgiveness is important."

After Mick left, Luke was antsy. He flitted from room to room, task to task, and finally decided he had to get out of the house. He gave Maria a quick call, found the set of keys she'd given him, and headed to her cottage on Keuka Lake.

Remembering how Jayne had loved the summer beauty of the hills and foliage of the Finger Lakes region as he drove up, Luke knew he shouldn't go to the cottage because it would remind him of her. But after Mick's visit and their talk about forgiveness, Luke knew he needed to think about Jayne. And he wanted to do it at the lake, where they'd connected over Timmy.

He was right. Once inside the cottage, Luke was slammed with memories.

Of Jayne's sincere offer to leave him alone if he needed solitude…of Jayne kneeling before him on the porch…of her face when he gave her little Hattie…and of her violet eyes sparkling like jewels when he asked her to move in with him.

He'd lost so much, so damned much.

Deciding to take the boat out, he went hunting for fishing gear. His father had taught him to fish when Luke was just a boy. It was their time together, and his dad had shown him the mechanics of the sport, but also, by example, how to use the quiet time to figure things out. Luke packed up the equipment, sped to deeper waters, and sat in the boat, watching the water lap, holding the pole, feeling the sun beating down on him.

And willingly thinking about Jayne.

She'd gone out on the lake with him. She went down below and made love to him with feelings that couldn't be faked. All weekend long, she gave of herself generously. Every single one of her actions during those four days had proved she'd cared deeply for him.

Instead of feeling worse at acknowledging that, though, Luke was buoyed by the thought and went back to the cottage with a lighter heart and ordered a pizza. As he was waiting for the delivery, he spotted the computer on the desk.

He never used the Internet anymore, but he was drawn to it tonight. When the machine booted up, the first thing he did was search Scarborough Associates. He read about the firm, Scarborough himself, and what kind of operation he ran. It was top-notch. Jayne could fit in there, regain her reputation and do the work she loved.

With another man!

While Luke was online, something made him do a search for Madison Conglomerates, the construction firm he used to work for, which was also in Manhattan. Though Elizabeth and Luke had ended badly, he recalled Granger Madison's last words to him during his exit interview.

I can't tell you how sorry I am about Tim O'Malley. I understand why you'd want to get away from all this. If I can ever do anything for you, let me know.

The company was prospering, too, despite the economy. Hmm, Elizabeth was vice president of sales. That was new. They were planning several projects. He noted one in particular, a concert hall for a local college. An architect hadn't been hired yet.

Luke sighed. Leaning back in the chair, he stared at the screen a long time, contemplating what to do next.

JAYNE WOKE with a start and felt the other side of the bed. She was breathing hard, and tried to take in air. When her eyes adjusted, she recognized the decor—the four-poster bed, the high dressers and armoire in dark wood, the heavy window treatments. This wasn't Luke's bedroom—no skylights letting in the stars, no breezy windows. She was in her father's New York apartment— still sleeping in the spare room—and Luke hadn't told her loved her and everything was going to be okay.

It had been another dream.

Bereft, she sank back into the pillows. Damn, she was sick of feeling so bad. It had been a few days since she'd found out her license had been restored, and she should be on top of the world.

But she wasn't. For some reason, good news made her miss Luke more, had her analyzing their separation and her part in it. Sometimes, like now, she couldn't believe she'd walked out on him when he needed her the most.

You're a runner, he'd said.

Was she, still?

Throwing off the sheets, she grabbed her laptop off the corner desk, got back in bed and booted up the machine. Without analyzing what she was doing, without being strong, she called up her e-mail, ignored Jess's correspondence and hit New Message.

She typed in Luke's e-mail address.

And wrote:

Dear Luke,
It's the middle of the night. I just dreamed about you. I don't know why I'm writing this. Maybe to say I'm sorry about Cal. That he's in bad shape.
And to apologize that I left you when he'd been hurt. It was so wrong and I can't believe I did that to you.
Jayne

"Delete it," she told herself as she stared at the blinking cursor. "You shouldn't be apologizing, he should."

But even as she said the words aloud, she knew they weren't true. She'd been wrong, too, as she said in the note. And although nothing could bring the two of them back together, at least she could be honest with him and maybe they could part friends.

She pressed Send and went back to bed. For the first time in weeks, she fell right to sleep.

LUKE SLEPT at the cottage and in the morning called Jess to say he wouldn't be at the site that day. He felt good about what he'd done last night, but he needed more time to work things through in his mind. He had to check his e-mail, though, regarding some orders he and Jess had put in, so he went to the computer and called up his account. There was a message from Granger Madison that he was about to click on, but right beneath it was another that caught his eye—from JLogan@ LoganAssociates.com. He froze.

Then deflated. So, things had been put in the works already? He checked his watch. It was late enough for her to know. Jayne was e-mailing him about what he'd done. So why did he feel bad?

Because he wished she'd contacted him before he made the first move. It would mean something totally different.

Still, he clicked into the missive, which was an apology for walking out on him when Cal was hurt. Luke scrutinized every inch of the e-mail, trying to read between the lines, but there was nothing there.

His gaze landed on the time it was sent.

Three o'clock in the morning.

This morning.

It took him a minute, then he grinned for the first time in weeks. "Well, I'll be damned."

JAYNE HURRIED into Scarborough Associates with a spring in her step. She'd overslept and was late getting here. But she felt good this morning. She didn't know if it was because she'd reached out to make peace with Luke, or because she'd gotten her license back, or what it was. In any case, she was humming as she walked down the corridor.

Ben stepped out of his office into the hall, as if he'd

been waiting for her. "Jayne, could you come in here, please?"

"Sure." She was still smiling when she went inside and found Ben wasn't alone. Seated on his big leather couch was the most beautiful woman Jayne had ever seen.

Mounds of dark hair flowing down her back.

Dressed in a gorgeous yellow Armani suit.

Eyes, skin of a model.

Jayne said, "Hello."

"Hello, Jayne,"

That was odd. Jayne didn't know this person. She'd remember meeting someone so striking.

"Jayne, this is Elizabeth Madison."

Elizabeth Madison? *Madison!* "I'm sorry, did we know each other when I worked for your company?"

"No, I wasn't on staff then. I'm a friend of Luke Corelli's."

Oh, dear God, this was *Elizabeth,* Luke's former fiancée. Jayne's good mood changed to nervousness. And something else...jealousy.

"Have a seat," Ben said, and when she did, continued, "Elizabeth is here as a representative of Madison Conglomerates. She's come to offer you a job."

"A job?"

"Our company is building a concert hall for SUNY Purchase. We want you to design it. My father says you did a good job for us years ago." She nodded to Ben. "Scarborough Associates will supervise, of course, given what's happened to you recently, but the job's yours if you want it."

Briefly, Jayne glanced at Ben. "Is this *your* doing?"

But Elizabeth answered. "No, it's Luke's. He contacted my father early last evening."

"Luke did this? Why?"

"To call in a favor. Daddy admired and respected Luke. And we all felt bad about Tim O'Malley. My father told Luke if he ever needed anything…." She trailed off as if Jayne should be able to finish her sentence.

"I don't understand."

"Apparently Luke's still riding his white horse. He called asking Madison Conglomerates to give you a chance to prove yourself again in the architecture world." She shrugged a delicate shoulder. "Daddy said yes."

"I see."

"Do you? I came here myself to find out exactly what kind of woman could bring Luke to ask us for a favor. To my knowledge, he's never done anything that resembled groveling before."

Something was niggling at Jayne. "When did you say he called?"

"About six last night."

A small smile blossomed inside Jayne. She'd written the e-mail in the early hours of the morning. And Luke had made the call to get her a job with Madison Conglomerates before he'd received her peace offering.

AFTER JAYNE'S E-MAIL:
    Day 1

Dear Luke,
I had a visit from Elizabeth Madison this morning. Thank you so much for getting me the opportunity to work with Madison Conglomerates again. The job will go a long way toward restoring my professional reputation. I don't know what to say to com-

municate how grateful I am. I don't know what to say about a lot of things.
Jayne

Dear Jayne,
You're welcome. I know you'll do well for them. I can't find words either about what happened.
Luke

Day 2

Dear Luke,
I've been thinking about this for a day. Does your recommendation mean you trust my judgment, my professional ability? I really want to believe that.
Jayne

Dear Jayne,
Believe it! I was an ass to think otherwise and got caught up in my stupid save-the-day mentality. I'm so sorry for that, for not trusting your competence, for not believing you.
Regretfully,
Luke

Day 3

Dear Luke,
I accept your apology. I hope you've accepted mine. I can't believe things turned out so badly between us.
Warmly,
Jayne

Dear Jayne,
I did accept yours. That's not why I called Granger
Madison. And I can't believe what happened to us,
either.
Warmly, too. (Sometimes a lot.)
Luke

Dear Luke,
I know that's not why you did it. I figured out the
timing. How about that?
Yours,
Jayne

Day 4

Dear Jayne,
☺How about that!☺
Yours, too.
Luke

Dear Luke,
Is everything okay with your family? Is Cal doing better?
Yours, always,
Jayne

Dear Jayne,
Cal's in A.A. Corky's sticking around for the time
being. Relationships go through bad times, and
survive, I guess. Don't you think?
Hopefully,
Luke

Dear Luke,
Yes, I do! I really do!
How are *you*?
Thinking of you a lot,
Jayne

Dear Jayne,
I'm rotten. I miss you.
Thinking of you, too. All the time,
Luke

Dear Luke,
I miss you, too. So much it hurts.
Thinking of you all the time,
Jayne

   Day 6

Dear Jayne,
It's midnight. I'm missing you more than ever. What
do you have on right now?
Luke, very hot

Dear Luke,
What do I have on?
Hmm, come see for yourself.
Jayne, in the same boat

   Luke almost dropped his laptop on the floor as he
bounded out of bed, dragged on the jeans and a T-shirt
he'd tossed on a chair earlier and glanced at the clock.

It was 12:20 a.m. If he drove fast, he could get to New York in four hours.

Searching for his shoes, his mind whirled. Should he let her know what he was doing? No, he was afraid she'd have second thoughts and tell him not to come.

What would he need? Phone, keys, wallet. Oh, and the code to her father's apartment. He jogged down-stairs to the basement and found the boxes of New York stuff he'd packed away. It took him a half hour to rifle through them and get what he needed. He left the basement a mess, but finally, finally, his life was getting back on track.

STILL NO RESPONSE.

Feeling like an idiot, Jayne sat before the computer with a heavy heart. It had been a half hour since she sent the message and Luke hadn't e-mailed her back. She'd jumped the gun, acted too rashly by telling Luke to come to her. Oh, God, why had she been so spontaneous?

Because he'd always encouraged her to go with her heart. And because she was in love with him. Their e-mail exchange this past week had given her hope, given them both time to test the waters, and Jayne had realized that without him, nothing meant much in her life. Damn it, she *hadn't* made a mistake by making the overture. It was time to tell Luke outright how she felt. It was time to stop running.

And if he wouldn't come to her, she'd go to him. She'd tie things up here in New York tomorrow and drive to Riverdale to face Luke in person. She'd stay until she convinced him that they were good together and could make their relationship work. Her fear of trusting someone had been diluted by her feelings for Luke.

With the comfort of that thought, Jayne went back to bed. But she couldn't fall asleep. She was too excited, too nervous, and now that she'd admitted it, let herself feel it, she wanted Luke more than anything in the world. Even more than another chance to make her way in architecture.

At dawn, she got up and threw on a robe to cover the peach-colored camisole and tap pants—why hadn't she just told him she was wearing something provocative and played the sex angle better? She made coffee and was sipping it, watching the sun come up over the city, when a knock on the apartment door startled her.

No one could get inside the building and up to the apartment but her mother or father, who had the code. She hoped nothing was wrong.

Rushing to the foyer, she flung open the door and was shocked to find a very disreputable looking Luke standing in the hall. His clothes were wrinkled, he was unshaven, his eyes were bloodshot.

And he'd never looked better.

In typical Luke style, he gave her a once-over—the robe gaped open—and a smile curved the corners of his beautiful mouth. "Oh, man. Look at you."

She bit her lip so she wouldn't cry. "I told you to come see."

"And I came." He rolled his eyes. "Through god-awful construction and a gale force rainstorm. I'm even double-parked so my car will probably get towed." Without waiting for an invitation, he stepped inside and shut the door.

And Jayne threw herself at him. He held on to her. "I'm sorry," and "I'm so sorry," they said at once.

No more words. They just held each other, eyes closed, clasped tight.

After a few moments, Luke pulled back. His dark eyes glowed with suppressed emotion. "Want to talk first?" he asked hoarsely.

"No, take me to bed, then we'll talk."

Needing little encouragement, Luke picked her up and headed straight for the master bedroom, cradling her close to his heart. She clung to him, nuzzled into him, inhaled the scent that had haunted her nights.

On the drive down, Luke had promised himself that he wouldn't rush her, that he'd take his time and gently woo her back to him, just like the first time they'd made love. But already his body was raging with need and he was feeling his control slip.

He managed to set her on the bed and sit next to her. Very slowly, he slid the robe off her shoulders, revealing bare skin that made his heart stop and his erection harder than granite. Still, he tugged at the strap of her teddy tenderly. It fell to the side and, leaning over, he kissed her silky skin, its texture and scent making him so aroused he could barely stand it. "I missed this spot right here," he whispered at the crook of her neck.

"Luke, please…"

With hands that were now shaking, he drew the other strap down, then the teddy itself. Leaning in, bending his head, his mouth closed over a bared nipple. She bucked, grabbed the back of his neck. "Luke…"

"I want to go slow, to savor. I won't hurry you. Into anything." A quick nip. "I promise, sweetheart. I'm done fixing things."

"No, no, not slow. I need you now."

When he continued the gentle assault, she played dirty. She moved her hand to the fly of his jeans and pressed hard. "What the…shit, Jayne."

She kept it up, yanking at the zipper until, to protect himself, he had to lean back. She freed him and took him between both her palms. He almost ricocheted off the bed.

"That's it," he said, standing abruptly and dragging off his jeans, then bending over to pull at the hem of her camisole. After he got it over her head, she leaned forward and put her mouth on him.

"Damn it, Jayne," he said when he saw her siren's smile. She knew exactly what she was doing.

After rolling on a condom so roughly he winced, he reached for her tap pants and was sorry they ripped, but he couldn't help himself. Covering her body, locking their eyes, he plunged into her. She cried out and arched her hips forward. It only took two more thrusts and she came, fast and furious. Before she even finished, he followed suit.

After a couple of minutes of blissful oblivion, Luke managed to roll off her.

Jayne liked Luke's weight on her, but was feeling so boneless, she couldn't move to hold him in place. He drew her to his chest, where she cuddled willingly.

Neither said anything for a very long time.

Finally, he spoke. "I don't know if I can ever make this all up to you, but I want to try."

"I feel the same," she confided, kissing his collarbone. "We were both wrong."

"We can do it, sweetheart. I can win your trust back, and forget about what you did."

"Maybe we shouldn't forget, Luke. People make mistakes, like somebody very wise told me when I found out I'd caused the Coulter collapse." She ran her hand over his pecs. "We made bad ones with each other.

You didn't believe me and I was heartless to leave when you'd just gotten such bad news. Let's acknowledge them and go on."

"All right." He rubbed her arm up and down, his callused fingers making her skin tingle. "And I've changed my mind about the job with Madison Conglomerates. You can't join Scarborough Associates. You have to come back to Riverdale and work with me. You can be the architect for Harmony Housing, we'll get the dog from Jess and Naomi—who are doing great, by the way—and we'll live together in my house."

Jayne chuckled. "I can see how much you've changed, how you aren't going to fix things anymore."

He chuckled. "Sorry."

"I'll do what you ask on one condition."

"Anything."

"That you marry me."

"Hell, darlin', I was just going to propose."

They both laughed.

"I think we skipped a step, though," he said.

Dreamily, she asked, "What was that?"

Moving over her again, he braced his elbows on either side of her head and brushed his knuckles over her cheek. He stared directly into her eyes, his shining like cat's-eye marbles. "I love you, Jayne Logan. It's been a damned crazy path that got us here, but I love you with all my heart."

"Oh! I love you too. Very, very much."

Again the sexy smile. "Good. Now that that's settled, it's time for round two." His lower body pressed into her and she felt him swell against her.

"Whatever you say, Luke."

"Yeah, like hell." He grinned at her, added, "But for now, I'll accept that," and began kissing his way down her body.

* * * * *

RICK'S APPOINTMENT with his attorney early Wednesday morning went only moderately better than his meeting with social services the day before. The prognosis wasn't great—but at least his attorney was going to file a motion for DNA testing. Just so Rick could petition to see the child…his sister's baby. The sister he didn't know he had until it was too late.

The rest of what his attorney said had been downhill from there.

Cell phone in hand before he'd even reached his Nitro, Rick punched in the speed dial number he'd programmed the day before.

Maybe foster parent Sue Bookman hadn't received his message. Or had lost his number. Maybe she didn't want to talk to him. At this point he didn't much care what she wanted.

"Hello?" She answered before the first ring was complete. And sounded breathless.

Young and breathless.

"Ms. Bookman?"

"Yes. This is Rick Kraynick, right?"

"Yes, ma'am."

"I recognized your number on caller ID," she said, her voice uneven, as though she was still engaged in whatever physical activity had her so breathless to begin with. "I'm sorry I didn't get back to you. I've been a little…distracted."

The words came in more disjointed spurts. Was she jogging?

"No problem," he said, when, in fact, he'd spent the better part of the night before watching his phone. And fretting. "Did I get you at a bad time?"

"No worse than usual," she said, adding, "Better than some. So, how can I help?"

God, if only this could be so easy. He'd ask. She'd help. And life could go well. At least for one little person in his family.

It would be a first.

"Mr. Kraynick?"

"Yes. Sorry. I was…are you sure there isn't a better time to call?"

"I'm bouncing a baby, Mr. Kraynick. It's what I do."

"Is it Carrie?" he asked quickly, his pulse racing.

"How do you know Carrie?" She sounded defensive, which wouldn't do him any good.

"I'm her uncle," he explained, "her mother's— Christy's—older brother, and I know you have her."

"I can neither confirm nor deny your allegations, Mr. Kraynick. Please call social services." She rattled off the number.

"Wait!" he said, unable to hide his urgency. "Please," he said more calmly. "Just hear me out."

"How did you find me?"

"A friend of Christy's."

"I'm sorry I can't help you, Mr. Kraynick," she said softly. "This conversation is over."

"I grew up in foster care," he said, as though that gave him some special privilege. Some insider's edge.

"Then you know you shouldn't be calling me at all."

"Yes… But Carrie is my niece," he said. "I need to see her. To know that she's okay."

"You'll have to go through social services to arrange that."

"I'm sure you know it's not as easy as it sounds. I'm a single man with no real ties and I've no intention of petitioning for custody. They aren't real eager to give me the time of day. I never even knew Carrie's mother. For all intents and purposes, our mother didn't raise either one of us. All I have going for me is half a set of genes. My lawyer's on it, but it could be weeks—months—before this is sorted out. Carrie could be adopted by then. Which would be fine, great for her, but then I'd have lost my chance. I don't want to take her. I won't hurt her. I just have to see her."

"I'm sorry, Mr. Kraynick, but…"

* * * * *

Find out if Rick Kraynick will ever have a chance to meet his niece.
Look for A DAUGHTER'S TRUST
by Tara Taylor Quinn,
available in September 2009.

**We'll be spotlighting a different series
every month throughout 2009
to celebrate our 60th anniversary.**

**Look for Harlequin® Superromance®
in September!**

*Celebrate with
The Diamond Legacy
miniseries!*

Follow the stories of four cousins as they come to terms
with the complications of love and what it means to
be a family. Discover with them the sixty-year-old secret
that rocks not one but two families.

A DAUGHTER'S TRUST by *Tara Taylor Quinn*
September

FOR THE LOVE OF FAMILY by *Kathleen O'Brien*
October

LIKE FATHER, LIKE SON by *Karina Bliss*
November

A MOTHER'S SECRET by *Janice Kay Johnson*
December

Available wherever books are sold.

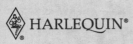

HARLEQUIN®

American ★ Romance®

The Ranger's Secret
REBECCA WINTERS

When Yosemite Park ranger Chase Jarvis rescues
an injured passenger from a downed helicopter,
he is stunned to discover it's the woman he
once loved. But Chase is no longer the man
Annie Bower knew. Will she forgive him for
the secret he's been keeping for ten long years?
And will he forgive Annie for her own secret—
the daughter Chase didn't know he had…?

*Available September
wherever books are sold.*

"LOVE, HOME & HAPPINESS"

www.eHarlequin.com

HA375279

HARLEQUIN *SuperRomance*

COMING NEXT MONTH

Available September 8, 2009

#1584 A DAUGHTER'S TRUST • Tara Taylor Quinn
The Diamond Legacy
As if the news of a sixty-year-old love triangle wasn't enough to upset
Sue Bookman's life, Rick Kraynick wants custody of his niece—Sue's beloved
foster baby. And he appears to have designs on Sue....

#1585 HER SO-CALLED FIANCÉ • Abby Gaines
Those Merritt Girls
Only sheer desperation could make Sabrina Merritt tell everyone she's going to marr
Jake Warrington...before he even pops the question! She knows her ex hates her, but
Sabrina—aka Miss Georgia—needs Jake. And the governor front-runner needs *her.* It
a win-win. Until their fake engagement turns into something more.

#1586 THE BABY ALBUM • Roz Denny Fox
9 Months Later
A lie is no way to start a job. Yet how can Casey Sinclair possibly tell her new boss
she's pregnant? Wyatt's still mourning the loss of his wife and unborn child. But as th
get closer, how long can she keep her secret?

#1587 SIMON SAYS MOMMY • Kay Stockham
The Tulanes of Tennessee
Dr. Ethan Tulane is in over his head. He's the new chief of surgery. He's learning to b
a dad to his adopted son. And he might have a thing for the nanny, Megan Rose. Can
convince her this temporary gig could be permanent?

#1588 FINDING THEIR SON • Debra Salonen
Spotlight on Sentinel Pass
Eli Robideaux appearing in her store to "borrow" money is not the reunion Char Jone
imagined. But now seems the right time to tell him about the son they created—the s
who could be the missing piece of their lives.

#1589 HERE TO STAY • Margot Early
Everlasting Love
Elijah Workman thought he and Sissy could conquer anything together—their differe
backgrounds, an autistic son, a house full of dogs. Then Elijah discovers their firstbo
isn't his son. Will the truth set them free to rebuild their marriage or will it ruin
everything?

HSRCNMBPA0809